COME BACK, STRANGER

Luke Matson, disturbed by a gunshot, finds a woman tending an unconscious rancher, Felix Wilson. When the bushwhacker returns, Matson bluffs him into believing that Wilson is already dead. In quick succession, Felix's father, a liveryman, and an old-timer are murdered, and Matson joins the sheriff and the Wilsons in an attempt to find the killers. Matson's gunplay and the sheriff's experience ought to be able to unravel the mystery, but before that can happen much blood will be spilt.

Books by Al Joyson
in the Linford Western Library:

GUN-TOTING DRIFTER
MORGAN TAKES A HAND

AL JOYSON

COME BACK, STRANGER

Complete and Unabridged

LINFORD
Leicester

First published in Great Britain in 2000 by
Robert Hale Limited
London

First Linford Edition
published 2001
by arrangement with
Robert Hale Limited
London

British Library CIP Data

Joyson, Al
    Come back, stranger.—Large print ed.—
Linford western library
    1. Western stories
    2. Large type books
    I. Title
    823.9'14 [F]

ISBN 0–7089–5971–7

Published by
F. A. Thorpe (Publishing)
Anstey, Leicestershire

Set by Words & Graphics Ltd.
Anstey, Leicestershire
Printed and bound in Great Britain by
T. J. International Ltd., Padstow, Cornwall

This book is printed on acid-free paper

1

At the sound of the shot, Luke Matson's right hand dropped automatically to his belt. He shook his head ruefully. It had been long years since he had carried a Colt. But now, before the echoes of the shot died away, a woman screamed, and the harsh sound brought relentless pictures spilling back momentarily into his mind.

Silence. And then in the growing dark the sound of a horse breaking into a gallop. Now the woman again. Sounds harsher than the scream. Sobs. He felt his body stiffen. His hand slapped senselessly at the empty belt.

Then, soft into his mind came again the pain-filled voice from the past. 'No more, Luke. No more killing.' And the barely audible last words. 'Not for me . . . Promise . . . '

But she had never heard his answer.

1

A vow he had kept for ten dark years. It had not been easy. In places where his name was still known and feared there had been many looking for another rung in the gunman's ladder to instant fame. By the time his empty belt was accepted without taunts, his fists had become almost as notorious as his forty-five had been.

But he was ten years older now. He cleared his mind of everything but the plight of the woman whose sobs he could still hear, and urged his horse slowly forward. At last he could make out two forms on the ground at the side of the trail. One was kneeling, and he could dimly see that it was a woman, bending over a motionless man. Two horses stood quietly nearby.

He dismounted. At that moment the moon cleared the bank of dark clouds and he saw her face, saw the lines of sorrow, the closed eyes. Without thinking, he bent and placed a hand on her shoulder.

She shuddered, her eyes still closed.

Without turning, she spoke. Her voice was cold and calm. 'You've killed him, Pallas. What are you going to do now — kill me, so there'll be no witness?'

Taken by surprise, he said nothing. He took his hand away, conscious of the fact that she was young, and that the moonlight was lacing the soft strands of her dark hair with gold that emphasized the sad hollows of her face as she bent over the still figure.

And then he saw something else. The fingers of the man's right hand slowly opened and then shut again. Matson said quietly, 'I'm not Pallas. An' your friend's not dead.'

She opened her eyes then. They were wide with disbelief. 'He's not breathing. He's been shot in the chest. And who are you?'

Her companion's face was a bloodless mask; his eyes were closed. Matson ignored the question. He got to his feet and walked across to his horse. He pulled down a canteen, went back, and then held the canteen to the man's lips.

His eyes were still unopened, but at last he managed to gulp a mouthful of water.

Matson looked at the girl.

'He was lucky,' he said. 'Mebbe the light was goin', or he moved a little jest as the *hombre* fired.' He went down on his knees for a closer look. He whistled softly. 'Lucky's not the word. Two inches lower an' he would've been very dead. Looks like the slug went straight through. But whoever fired the shot must've reckoned he was dead.'

In the now-clear moonlight her face was still full of suspicion.

'But how do I — ' She broke off suddenly. 'You're not wearing a gun. I'm sorry. But I thought Felix was dead. And then you turned up.'

'I heard a shot,' he said. 'An' yuh were screaming.'

Her eyes opened wide. 'But you're not wearing a gun. Why did you stop? You could have got yourself killed.'

It was a good question. What good could he have done if the bushwhacker had seen him? Embarrassed, he could think of nothing to say. He was relieved when the wounded man suddenly struggled to sit up. He bent over him. 'Take it easy, son. Don't try to move yet.'

The man's eyes opened. His right hand moved haltingly towards his gun-belt, but gave up the attempt half way. 'Why'd yuh plug me?' he demanded shakily. 'I ain't ever seen yuh before.' His eyes closed.

Matson looked at the girl. 'He needs a doctor, ma'am.'

She nodded. 'I'll fetch one.' She hesitated. 'Could you wait till I get back, Mr . . . ?'

'Matson. Luke Matson, ma'am.' He smiled at her. 'An' I'll wait.'

She said, 'I'm obliged to you, Mr Matson, I'm Susan Tate.'

Then she was in the saddle, half-turning, raising an arm in salute, and was gone.

Matson sat quietly by the side of the wounded man, who looked to be in his early twenties. He found out that his name was Felix Wilson, and that he and Susan Tate were neighbours, but after that the man's eyes closed and his breathing grew shallow. There was nothing Matson could do but wait. He was almost dozing, when a slight sound from nearby brought him to instant alertness.

Then he froze. A dim figure crouched among the bushes. A Winchester glinted in the moonlight. Stealthily Matson drew the Colt from Wilson's holster, telling himself there was nothing in his promise to stop him defending himself when his life was in danger. Perhaps someone had come back to finish a job.

The figure spoke. 'It ain't your quarrel, *hombre*. Supposin' yuh fork your bronc an' ride.' The voice was quiet, almost casual, but there was a flatness to it. The Winchester swung up, to line on the inert form of the wounded man.

The butt of the Colt seemed to mould into Matson's grip. He said slowly, 'What quarrel would yuh have with a dead man, *amigo*?' Tensely he waited for the slightest movement of the Winchester.

There was a silence. Then the figure seemed to melt into the surrounding features of the landscape, and was gone.

2

The moon half vanished behind the drifting clouds. In the shadows, Luke Matson quietly relaxed, but minutes passed before he slid Felix Wilson's Colt back into its holster. He had reckoned that in the half light it would be impossible for the intruder to tell that Wilson was still alive. It seemed his bluff had worked. Though the wounded man's survival could still depend on prompt attention from a doctor.

Time passed, once more the moon came into full view, and, almost an hour after Susan Tate had left, he heard the unmistakable sound of a buckboard in the distance.

Minutes later a stout figure pushed past him and knelt at Wilson's side. Susan Tate was with him. After a while the newcomer raised his head and glared at Matson. 'Who are you?' he demanded, bending down again and carrying on working.

'Name's Matson,' said Luke frostily, a little annoyed at the other's tone. 'What's yours?'

The man's head came up again with a jerk, and the beginnings of a smile seemed to reach his lips. 'Parkinson, Doc Parkinson from Baronsley. Which makes me a local man, Mr Matson, whereas you are, I think, a stranger.' His voice hardened. 'So, why are you here?'

Matson nodded in understanding. To a lot of people, the doctor's suspicions would make sense. Someone had been shot dead. A stranger was nearby when it happened. A ready-made suspect.

Susan Tate spoke for the first time. 'Mr Matson wasn't carrying a gun. He stopped to help Felix and me.'

The doctor said testily, 'He could have hidden it. Even thrown it away.'

The girl was insistent. 'I asked him to stay and look after Felix while I came to fetch you. He could have killed him and

9

been miles away by now. But he waited for us to come back.' She looked at Matson, and a sudden warm smile illuminated her face. 'I didn't doubt you'd be here, Mr Matson, and I'm grateful to you.'

'So am I,' said a weak voice from the ground. 'This *hombre* saved my life. The bushwhacker came back to finish me off, an' if Matson hadn't been here I'd have been a goner. Matson convinced him I was already dead — an' he vamoosed.'

The doctor said, 'No more talking, Felix. We've got to get you back home and into bed.' He stood up. 'Guess I owe you an apology, Matson.' Slowly and carefully his gaze travelled over him, 'No gun; no ammunition. I'm sorry. I spoke out of turn. Most strangers passing through Baronsley nowadays wear a gun. Some of them wear two.'

'I haven't carried a gun in ten years.' Matson spoke softly. He indicated the wounded man. 'I'll give yuh a hand, Doc.'

Together, they lifted Felix Wilson gently onto the buckboard. Matson hitched their horses to the back of the vehicle. Susan Tate picked up the reins.

The trail was rough and the buckboard had seen better days, but Doc Parkinson and Matson managed to save Wilson from the worst of the road's surface. Then half an hour later they turned off the main trail. Ahead of them buildings loomed up in the moonlight.

'It's the Wilson spread — the Bar W,' said the doctor, in answer to Matson's question.

At the ranch-house door, Susan halted the buckboard and ran up the porch steps. The door swung open and a short, wiry-looking man appeared. He seemed surprised.

'Where's Felix, Susan? I thought he was with you.'

She hesitated for a moment. Then she said softly, 'He is with me, Mr Wilson. I'm afraid he's been shot. Doc Parkinson's with him. Don't worry, he's going to be all right.' She pointed to the buckboard.

Wilson's features seemed to drain of colour in the lamplight. Then, as Matson watched, the rancher's face flamed with anger. His voice was savage. 'Rick Pallas! I'll bet my life on it!'

'You'd lose your money, Dad,' said an almost inaudible voice from the buckboard.

The rancher turned and took the steps two at a time.

When he reached the buckboard, Doc Parkinson put a hand on the little man's shoulder. 'Let's save the talking for later, John,' he suggested. 'He's going to be all right, but we need to get him indoors and into bed, pronto!' He looked at Luke. 'You've been a great help, Mr Matson. Will you give me a hand to get him inside?'

They carried Felix Wilson up the stairs and into his bedroom. The doctor bent over him. John Wilson hovered in the background with a white-faced girl whom he called Janet, and who was obviously his daughter. Matson looked at her, thinking that normally she would be a laughing, carefree girl. He watched the scene for a few moments and then quietly made his way down to the living-room.

Susan Tate looked up from her seat by the fire. Her face was pale. 'How's Felix?' she whispered.

'He's restin' now,' said Matson. He suddenly felt a stranger here in these surroundings. And this girl, sitting quietly by the fire, the flames making a rosy halo around her hair, spoke to him of another age, another life, of almost forgotten evenings with loved ones.

He was so lost in thoughts that at first he did not realize that John Wilson had come into the room.

The rancher said, 'Janet is stayin' with him now fer a while, Susan.' He turned to Matson and shook his hand warmly. 'I'm greatly obliged to yuh, Mr Matson. Doc reckons that if yuh hadn't stayed with Felix, the bushwhacker would have finished the job when he came back.'

Suddenly, Luke Matson felt ill at ease, an interloper here. All he had asked of life for so long had been a dull peace, a quiet anonymity. And now the warmth and friendliness of the people in this room surrounded him, enveloped him, almost choked him.

'It was nothin',' he said, shaking his head. 'Nothin'. I jest happened along. Now I'd best git goin'.'

'It's late, friend,' said John Wilson. 'We've plenty of room, an' you're more than welcome to stay the night.'

Another figure had come into the room. A small, plump woman, with bright eyes. An older version of Janet Wilson. She looked surprised, and then, suddenly uneasy. 'Something's happened, John? What is it?'

John Wilson put his hand on her shoulder. 'Yuh're not to start worryin', Martha, Felix's been hurt some, but Doc Parkinson and Janet are with him, an' he's goin' to be fine. An' Mr

14

Matson here did us all a service by helpin' when help was most needed.'

The woman turned blue eyes, that suddenly glistened too brightly, in Luke Matson's direction. 'I'm obliged to you, Mr Matson. John's right. It's late. Just give me a few minutes and I'll — I'll make up a bed. It's no trouble.'

Luke looked at her and shook his head as he saw the shock and fear in her eyes. 'Thank you kindly, Mrs Wilson. But I'm jest passin' through. I'm real glad I could be of some help to your son, but I best git goin'.'

She shook his hand warmly, but he could sense the relief in her voice as she thanked him once more.

Then she almost stumbled from the room, and he heard the quick sound of her feet on the stairs. John Wilson hurried after her.

'That was kind of you, Mr Matson.' Susan Tate's eyes had widened with sudden understanding. Her voice was soft and warm.

He felt a sense of near shame. He

15

had done nothing, he told himself again. But the memory was clear in his mind. For the first time in years he'd had a gun in his hand. And had been prepared to use it. Reason or no reason, vow or no vow — he'd been ready to use it. He recalled the feel of the Colt as his fingers closed around the butt. More than that, there had been tension and wariness — and readiness — as he watched the man with the Winchester. And, he finally admitted to himself, he'd experienced a strange sense of disappointment when his bluff had succeeded.

He looked at the girl. Then he realized what had been troubling him most. If he'd had to use the gun, he would have broken his promise. But, it had all depended on the action taken by the bushwhacker. If the man had lifted that Winchester a fraction of an inch — he would have been dead. Or Susan Tate and the Wilsons would have been mourning the quite needless death of Felix Wilson.

He turned to the girl. He shook his

16

head slowly. His voice was low, almost harsh. 'Goodnight, ma'am.'

* * *

An hour later Luke Matson eased his horse through Baronsley's Main Street, lit only by the glimmer of the occasional lamp. He dismounted at the town's livery stable, and led his horse inside. A door opened at the far end of the building and the stooped figure of a man appeared, yawning and rubbing his eyes. He nodded at Matson, but spent more time looking over his horse, finally nodding once more, but this time apparently in approval.

He stopped yawning. 'I'm buyin', friend,' he said.

Matson grinned at him. 'I ain't sellin'. I'm tired an' dry. Where can I git a bed fer the night an' a drink?'

'Jest round the corner. Hotel's on one side; the Lucky Chance's on the other.' He looked at Matson sympathetically. 'I'll see to your hoss, stranger.'

17

Matson flipped him a coin. 'I'm obliged, friend.'

He picked up his war bag and walked out into the night air. A few yards farther on, the street took a sharp bend. Practically on the bend was a side street. The hotel entrance beckoned him on one side, faced by the batwing doors of a saloon on the other. He mentally tossed a coin, lost the toss, and walked into the hotel.

The pasty-faced clerk at the desk looked up as he entered. Without a word he pushed a register and a key towards him.

Matson glanced at the room number, signed the register, turned and climbed the stairs. They led to a long, half-lit corridor. His room was near the far end. He went in, gave it a cursory glance, dropped his bag in a corner, and went out again, locking the door behind him.

He left the hotel, crossed the street, and pushed through the inviting batwing doors. Inside, the atmosphere was thick with tobacco smoke. Through the haze he made out a bar-room, plain but clean, with tables and chairs around the bar itself at the far end. Card games were in full swing, and few of the players looked up as he entered.

He made his way to the bar and found a space for himself. The barkeep, a tall, thin man with hollow cheeks and wispy hair, finally reached him. His lips hardly seemed to move.

'What'll it be, stranger?' His mouth closed with almost a snap.

'Whiskey.' Matson nodded his thanks as the glass was propelled towards him. He looked up at the sweating bar-tender. 'Join me,' he invited. 'Yuh look as if yuh could use a drink.'

The barkeep winced. 'Don't yuh know that whiskey is the invention of Satan?' he demanded. 'Shame on yuh. I remember my ol' grandmother sayin' to my poor ol' grandfather, 'The lips that touch likker shall never touch mine'. Mind yuh, the ol' feller didn't seem too bothered about that. An' now yuh come

in here atemptin' me? Shame on yuh.'
He licked his lips. 'Still, jest this once,
huh? Thank yuh kindly.' He half filled a
glass and raised it swiftly to his lips.

At that moment the batwing doors
swung open, and suddenly the level of
noise in the room seemed to die down.
The voice of the barkeep behind Matson
said softly, 'It's Rick Pallas. This one's
all bad, an' when he's been drinkin'
— like he's been all day — then he
don't like strangers, an' he's seen you,
mister. Turn round very slowly.'

Matson sighed. But he did as the
barkeep advised. He eased himself
around until his back was against the
bar, his glass in his hand.

Coming towards him was a heavily
built man with a swarthy, pockmarked
face. A Colt nestled, tied down, against
his right thigh. He came to a
stiff-legged halt opposite Matson.

Luke lifted his glass steadily to his
lips. He'd seen the type in many
bar-rooms in the course of his wander-
ings. They all seemed to have heavy

shoulders, huge limbs, and at least the beginnings of a paunch. And they all fought the same way. Brute strength and a total lack of science. But he noticed the tied-down six-gun, and his memory suddenly came into action. Pallas. That was the name Susan Tate had flung at him accusingly when he found her weeping over the wounded Felix Wilson, though Wilson himself had later absolved Pallas from blame.

'Where yuh from, *hombre*?' Pallas glared at him.

Matson drained his glass, and put it down carefully on the bar counter. 'Jest ridin' through.'

Pallas scowled and took a step nearer. 'You don't hear good, *hombre*. I asked where you're from.'

Matson eyed him. There was no way he was going to get out of this confrontation peacefully. His face broke into a smile. 'Ain't no damned business o' yours, *hombre*.' His smile deepened as he emphasized the last word.

Pallas rocked back on his heels.

Behind him, Matson heard a swift intake of breath from the barkeep. Pallas bellowed and grabbed Matson by the front of his shirt. Luke planted his right foot firmly behind Pallas's foot, swung his body from the waist, and smashed his left elbow into the big man's solar plexus, following up with a vicious right to the jaw as he swung back again.

Pallas lost his grip on Matson, tripped over his outstretched foot, and crashed to the saloon floor, eyes closed, fighting for breath.

Matson looked past him and around the room. Poker forgotten, the customers to a man had left their chairs and were on their feet, necks craned to take in all the action.

Behind Matson the barkeep whispered, 'Watch yourself, stranger!'

Pallas had struggled to sit upright, hand stretching down to his Colt. He mouthed words through his strangled gasps for breath. 'Go fer your hardware, *hombre*. You're a dead man!'

3

Matson whirled round to face the gunman, but Pallas had succeeded in drawing his Colt. Matson could see the other's finger tightening on the trigger.

From the batwing doors came the bark of a rifle. Pallas staggered, blood pouring from his right arm. His Colt clattered to the floor. Matson caught the play of lamplight on the star worn by a tall figure, a Winchester now hanging loosely in his hand. He came up to the bar, limping slightly, a gangling, long-limbed, middle-aged man, with clear grey eyes and a droopy moustache. Pallas, left hand clutching his right arm, cursed him solidly at each step he took.

'What in tarnation d'yuh think you're doin', Stephens?' he demanded, as the lawman reached him. 'It was him an' me. Sheriff or not, yuh keep out of it.'

The sheriff stooped and picked up

the fallen Colt. He looked at Pallas sourly. 'The thought o' yuh danglin' on a rope don't bother me none,' he said. 'But your friend here was doin' a real good job on yuh, jest with his hands. Only thing was, if you'd put a slug in him, it would've been murder — an' yuh would've hanged. I did yuh a favour Pallas, though it turns my stomach to admit it.' He swung round and indicated Matson. 'The stranger ain't wearin' no hardware.'

Pallas ignored him. Instead, he turned and snarled at Matson, who now leaned against the bar, freshly refilled glass in his hand.

'Yuh an' me ain't finished, *hombre*. Make sure you're totin' a six-gun next time we meet. Mebbe there'll be no interferin' John Law to save your ornery hide then.'

Matson regarded him levelly. He had always known that sooner or later circumstances might make it impossible for him to continue keeping his vow. This Pallas, he knew, would be only too

24

pleased to meet him again, weaponless, and preferably without witnesses. While he stayed in Baronsley he would have to be armed.

He grinned at the irate gunman. 'Mebbe, right now, you'd like to carry on where we left off,' he suggested.

Pallas's face purpled. But the sheriff stepped between them.

'There'll be no more fightin' tonight,' he said.

At that, to a slowly dying chorus of disappointment, the excitement subsided. The card players sat down; the barkeep was swamped anew by demanding voices. Pallas, still cursing angrily, pushed his way through the onlookers and out through the batwing doors.

Luke Matson looked at the lawman, and beckoned to the barkeep when the frenzy had died down. He smiled to himself; he had been in Baronsley for barely an hour, and in that short time had managed to acquire two friends and an enemy. And all he had been looking for was a quiet drink before bedtime. He glanced up to find the barkeep pushing a bottle and three glasses towards him and the sheriff.

'On the house, fellers,' said the barkeep. Then his voice dropped as he fashioned his features into a rigidly sober outline. 'Not that I'm recommendin' yuh an' this gentleman o' the law to become allies o' the Demon Drink. But jest this once, I reckon no harm'll be done.'

The sheriff half-filled two glasses. He raised the bottle again and looked hard at the barkeep. 'Who's the third glass for? Hang on. Don't tell me you're turnin' to hard drink, after all your preachin'.' He poured whiskey into the glass.

'I'm ashamed to admit it,' confessed the barkeep. 'But be fair, Sheriff. I got to sell the stuff. So how am I goin' to tell if it's good — like all my customers reckon — if I don't test it once in a while? Jest this once, huh?' He raised the whiskey glass.

The sheriff shook his head sadly.

'Don't listen to him,' he said to Matson. 'Folk reckon he drinks six out o' every dozen bottles he has in stock, jest to test 'em — an' he ain't thrown one out yet.'

'Good job he ain't an undertaker,' said Matson. 'I suppose he'd have to test his coffins — right to the bitter end.'

'If that was a guess, it was a good one,' said the lawman gravely. 'Talk is that his whiskey's actually embalmin' fluid, an' he gits a dollar a head for every one o' his customers that finishes up with the local undertaker, on account of they're already nicely pickled.'

Matson picked up his drink, sniffed it, and drained his glass. He smacked his lips appreciatively and grinned at the bartender. 'Real good-class embalmin' fluid,' he acknowledged. 'But I reckon I could've been a customer o' your undertaker, if it weren't fer you an' the sheriff. I'm obliged to both o' yuh.'

The barkeep was busy refilling the glasses. He looked up.

'Pallas is mean with a gun,' he said. 'But he most generally picks a fist fight when it comes to strangers. I ain't ever seen him beaten till tonight. Reckon that's why he went fer his shootin' iron.' He broke off and studied Matson's face. 'He ain't one to pull out. He'll be lookin' fer a showdown.'

The sheriff had also been regarding Matson closely. He accepted the drink the barkeep pushed towards him. His face was expressionless. Then it broke out into something like a smile.

'I allus like to know the name of anyone I'm drinkin' with,' he said. 'I'm Pat Stephens.' He indicated the barkeep. 'An' this here gent is known far an' wide as Bud Jenning.'

Matson took the polite hint. He raised his glass to the pair of them. 'Matson,' he said quietly. 'Luke Matson.'

The sheriff nodded in a satisfied kind of manner. 'Yuh ever been in Dodge, Mr Matson?'

Matson looked at the older man, but there was nothing in his expression that

28

conveyed anything but a casual question. 'A few months, three, four years ago,' he said.

'I was jest passin' through, round about the same time,' said the sheriff. 'One day I saw two cow-punchers bad-talk a young feller on account of he didn't carry a gun. Judgin' by what he did to the pair of 'em, he didn't have much need o' one.' He looked hard at Matson. 'Pallas, now, he'd back-shoot yuh from ambush, an' then swear on a stack o' Bibles that yuh were carryin' more hardware than a troop o' cavalry.' He stopped, looking as if he was going to say more, but had then decided against it.

'Pat's right about Pallas,' said the barkeep. 'Ain't no business o' mine, but I reckon you'd be wise to pack a six-shooter. Yuh can't beat the hell out of a man with your fists if he's a hundred yards away an' hidin' in the bushes.'

At that moment the barkeep was called to the bar by a chorus of raucous insults from customers all allegedly dying of galloping dehydration.

The sheriff settled back in his chair and lifted his glass. 'Bud's a good barkeep — an' honest,' he said. 'The two things don't allus go together.'

Matson nodded. He had formed the same opinion of the bartender. He grinned at the lawman. 'An' Pallas. What about him?'

'Pallas ain't no laughin' matter,' said the lawman severely.

Matson thought of the events of the evening. He looked at Stephens. 'Reckon I should put you wise to what happened earlier tonight.'

Stephens reached for the bottle and refilled their glasses. 'I thought it had been very quiet, until I came in an' found you an' Pallas tanglin',' he said.

'I heard his name before I reached town,' said Matson. He went on to give the sheriff details of his encounter with Felix Wilson and the mystery gunman.

'An' Wilson was sure it wasn't Pallas

who bushwhacked him?' asked the sheriff.

'That's what he said. On the other hand he didn't say who it was.'

The sheriff frowned. 'Mebbe he doesn't know. Or mebbe he does know an' he chooses to make a personal thing of it. Ain't many men around here who could outgun Felix Wilson on an even break.' He looked at Matson slyly. 'Mind yuh, I've seen some who could — that young feller in Dodge fer instance. Before he gave up packin' a six-shooter.'

Matson downed his drink. The sheriff had glanced at him several times before, as though he was trying hard to place him. That had stopped when Matson gave him and the barkeep his name.

'Yuh've a good memory, friend,' Luke said softly. 'An' he ain't carried a gun since — but times change, an' I reckon now he'll have to.'

'I'm glad to hear you say that,' said Stephens. 'Because, if it ain't Pallas who's responsible, someone else is likely to reckon yuh took sides — knowin' or not — in a private quarrel. An' bushwhackers as a rule don't care if their targets are unarmed. Most of 'em would be quite happy to wait until that's the case.'

He sat back and looked around the room. 'Gittin' late. Yuh got somewhere to stay, Luke?'

'I booked in at the hotel,' said Matson. He waved away the offer of a refill. 'How could a stranger like me take sides in a private quarrel, Sheriff?'

'It's a bit complicated,' said Stephens. 'Come down to my office in the mornin', an' I'll show you around — an' fill in some o' the details.'

He got to his feet and Matson joined him. To Luke's surprise, the lawman insisted on escorting him not only to the hotel but also to his room. As they walked along the corridor of the second-floor bedrooms he seemed suddenly alert, and stepped quickly in front of Matson.

One of the doors had opened at the end of the corridor, and two figures appeared. In the dim light, Matson recognized the second man as Rick Pallas.

Stephens relaxed, but a scowl appeared an his rugged features.

In the narrow passage, the newcomer seemed huge, his eyes sullen, half-hidden in rolls of fat, thick lips twisted in a sneer. He looked Matson up and down, pausing at the sight of the empty belt. A thin mockery of a smile struggled briefly into life.

The sheriff said icily, 'Yuh want to share the joke, Ingham?'

The fat man froze, his left hand creeping downwards towards his Colt. Then slowly the hand rose again. When he spoke, his voice was a low-pitched hoarse growl. 'Not with yuh. Not while you're still Sheriff. Rick here ain't figurin' on joinin' in, neither.'

Pallas stayed silent. But Luke Matson saw the hate that flared briefly in the swarthy face.

Then Ingham had turned away to retrace his path down the corridor, calling roughly to Pallas to come with him. With an oath, Pallas turned on his heel and followed.

Luke Matson noticed that the sheriff stayed motionless, one hand near his gunbelt, until the two figures disappeared from view. The lawman kept his gun hand ready, also, as he found Luke's room number and eased the door open, stepping quietly inside, motioning Matson to stay still on the threshold.

The sheriff walked unhurriedly around the dimly lit room, stopping only to close the curtains before turning up the lamp. He stood still, looking and listening, and then, apparently satisfied, beckoned to Matson to come in.

Matson did so, closing the door behind him. At the foot of the bed he sat down and took a canvas-covered bundle from his bag. He unrolled it slowly and took out the weapon and belt it contained. He nodded in satisfaction at its condition, punched in shells, and slid the Colt into its holster.

He grimaced at the sheriff. 'Ain't my wish. But accordin' to you an' Bud it's plumb necessary.'

The sheriff looked hard at him. 'The story I heard in Dodge was that you had promised your wife not to kill anyone in revenge fer her death — it was an accident, an' she reckoned she had seen too many killings.'

Luke Matson was silent for a moment. Then he said, 'Yuh heard right.'

The lawman rolled a cigarette. He looked at Matson, who shook his head. Stephens struck a match, inhaled deeply, and seemed lost in thought.

Matson found that he was beginning to have a high regard for this man. He kept thinking of the way Stephens had stepped in front of him when they met Ingham and Rick Pallas in the corridor, no doubt to protect him because he was not armed. That had been the final incident which had persuaded him to carry a six-gun again after what now seemed a lifetime.

He said slowly, 'Yes, yuh heard right. But tonight, if Pallas or his sidekick — or both of 'em — had gone fer his hawgleg, you'd have thought it your duty to shoot it out with them because I wasn't carryin' a gun. That ain't ever happened to me before, an' it seems to me now that, as a man who can handle a Colt, I've got a duty as well — a duty to protect myself an' not to expect anyone to put himself in danger jest to save my ornery skin.'

Stephens shook his head. 'You're right, up to a point. But this is my town, an' every citizen — or stranger jest passin' through — is entitled to feel safe under the law.' He grinned at Matson. 'An' one day, who knows, it may happen.'

'It happened tonight,' pointed out Matson. 'What d'yuh reckon those two *hombres* would've done if yuh hadn't been around? Invited me to a poker game?'

He stood up and walked across the room to the window, the sheriff at his side. He pulled aside the curtains. Across the street a solitary lamp blinked in the surrounding dark. Then he saw it. The glint of that lamp's light on a suddenly raised rifle barrel. He turned and hurled himself at the sheriff, and the two of them crashed to the floor as the window behind them shattered into a thousand fragments.

4

Matson was the first back on his feet. Behind him the sheriff cursed softly as he dragged himself upright. Then, Colt in hand, the lawman edged his way along the wall to the side of the window, dropping to one knee as he reached it. He rose cautiously and looked out.

'Street's empty,' he said finally. 'An' I'm obliged to yuh, friend.' He turned to the door. 'Seems someone jest don't take to you, somehow. Mebbe he found out you'd outsmarted him, when you hinted that Felix Wilson was already dead.'

Matson grinned at him. 'Could be someone with a grudge against yuh. That Pallas *hombre* sure don't look on yuh as a long-lost brother.'

The sheriff grunted. 'He ain't the only one. Sheriffs don't figure high on the lists of the best beloveds. Someday I'll have a sleepless night worryin' about that. Anyway, I don't reckon there'll be any more trouble tonight — what's left of it. But all the same, you're welcome to come down to the office an' git yourself some sleep.'

Matson picked up his bag and joined the sheriff in the corridor. Downstairs, the clerk looked up as they appeared. 'Some drunk shooting out a window?' He stifled a yawn.

Luke Matson nodded. 'Could be. Anyway, lots o' cold, night air in a room ain't good fer my delicate constitution. But thanks fer your concern, friend.'

The clerk stifled another yawn. Then he seemed to notice Matson's Colt. His face paled. 'You — you mean it wasn't a drunk?'

'Figure it fer yourself,' said Sheriff Stephens kindly. 'A drunk would've seen your office, all lit up, you sittin' at your desk — a perfect target. He ain't goin' to waste his shootin' skills on an empty upstairs room, is he? Would you?'

The clerk gulped.

Matson put his room key on the desk. 'Don't worry your head none. He ain't likely to come back. Well, not very likely.' He patted the now trembling clerk on the shoulder. 'Git that window mended. I'll want that room tomorrow night. I sure hope you're still around.'

He and the sheriff stood and stared at the white-faced clerk, shaking their heads slowly and sadly. Straight-faced, they pushed their way through the hotel entrance.

Fifty yards away from the door they turned and looked. As they did so, the lamp in the hotel office turned down to a glimmer.

★　★　★

Luke Matson opened his eyes, stretched, and stood up. The sheriff's office boasted a desk, a few chairs, and two bunks — one of which, the sheriff had informed him, was for the use of a deputy, when he considered a deputy was necessary. The sheriff's bunk was empty.

A battered clock on the office wall told him that it was eight o'clock. Sunlight poured through the office window. Quickly, Matson washed and put on his gunbelt and boots. The weight of the Colt at his hip tugged him back to reality and the events of the previous night. He drew the six-gun and tossed it from hand to hand, feeling once more the weight and balance, until the awkwardness disappeared. Finally, he holstered the weapon, and turned and drew, repeating the draw, faster and faster, until he was satisfied with the smoothness and speed.

The clock now said half past eight. He took his Stetson from the hatstand, and walked outside to the porch. The air was already warm, the sun strident in a clear sky. He sighed contentedly, sat down and leaned back against the wall, Stetson pulled down over his eyes.

The sheriff's voice disturbed his thoughts. 'Yuh goin' to sleep all day,

Luke, or d'yuh want some breakfast?'

Matson looked up. 'Breakfast? Hell, I knew I was missin' something.' He got to his feet and followed Stephens down Main Street. The lawman stopped outside a single-storey building. A sign proclaimed it to be Josey's Restaurant. Stephens pushed open the door and went in, Matson at his side.

The large airy room was furnished simply with a dozen small tables, two or four chairs to a table, obviously placed to get the maximum amount of light from the two large windows. Most of the tables were taken, their occupants not lifting their heads as the door opened.

'Grub must be good,' whispered Matson to the sheriff, as they came to an empty table.

'Ain't that a fact?' agreed Stephens, as they pulled up chairs and sat down. He had hardly got the words out of his mouth before a woman was at their table with two enormous plates of food, seemingly almost too large for her to carry. Matson smiled at her. She could not have been more than five foot tall, in her early forties at a guess, her hair still dark and luxuriant. Little laughter lines appeared at the corners of her brown eyes as she smiled back.

'You've got a choice of meal, stranger,' she said. 'What'll it be?'

'Josey means that as a stranger you've got a pick o' those two plates,' said the sheriff gravely. 'Which d'yuh want, left or right?'

Luke Matson studied the offered dishes. As far as he could see, they were identical. He picked the right-hand one.

To his amazement, the woman burst into a wild rebel yell, and slapped the sheriff on the back. 'Pay up, Pat!' she demanded.

The sheriff shook his head sadly, and pulled a coin from his pocket. 'That's the fourth or fifth time this year I've brought someone in here, Josey,' he said. 'An' I ain't ever beat yuh yet. This ain't a restaurant, it's a gamblin' den, an' I ought to close yuh down while I've still got a little *dinero* left.'

He turned to Matson. 'I would, too, but the grub's so good the citizens o' this town would probably string me up.'

'You talk too much, Pat,' said Josey, genially. 'Shut up and let him enjoy his breakfast before it gets cold, or I'll throw you out.'

'I git more threats in here than in Bud Jenning's bar,' groaned the sheriff, holding up his hands in mock supplication.

Matson looked up for a brief moment. 'I jest ain't got time,' he mumbled, 'to talk to yuh right now. This here grub's sure enough delicious.' He grinned as he realized that the sheriff was now following his example, and resumed his attack on his plate.

Back in his office after the meal, Sheriff Stephens produced a bottle of whiskey and two glasses. Without a word he poured out two stiff slugs, and passed one to Matson. 'What d'yuh think o' Josey?' he inquired as he raised his glass.

Matson smiled happily at him. 'If you're suggestin' we should raise our glasses to that lady, I'm right behind yuh,' he said, lifting his drink high. 'I ain't ever had a breakfast like that before.' He gave the sheriff a shrewd glance.

Stephens leaned back in his chair, quietly studying the whiskey in his glass. He sighed. 'Most lawmen ain't married. They'll tell yuh they ain't the marryin' kind. What they really mean is that the job's too uncertain to ask a woman to share their life.'

'It ain't jest her cookin', then?' asked Matson.

The sheriff shook his head. 'Josey came to Baronsley a couple o' years back, an' opened her restaurant. It went well, an' we seemed to hit it off, too. Every now an' again I think the time is right to ask her . . . ' He broke off and his face hardened. 'Then some so-called badman comes ridin' into town an' tells the world he was born with a Colt in his fist, an' jest naturally eats sheriffs fer breakfast, an' am I goin' to draw or is he goin' to shoot me down like a dawg? An' when I try to talk him out of it — he jest ain't listening.'

'An' Josey?' asked Matson gently.

'The next time I see her, she's got a frozen sort o' look, as if her world has suddenly stopped at a corner an' she daren't look round it to see what's goin' to happen next.'

The sheriff got to his feet. 'Hell, I'm talkin' too much about myself. Don't generally run on like this. But I'm worried about this town. Apart from the glory-hunters, it's been a peaceful sort o' place — until mebbe six months ago.'

Matson stood up and reached for his Stetson. 'What happened?' He followed Stephens out into the street.

The sheriff looked back over his shoulder. 'I can't put my finger on the trouble yet. Come on, I'll show yuh around town.' He laughed. 'Mebbe a stranger can spot somethin' I'm missin'.'

Luke Matson was not fooled by the laugh. The sheriff was a worried man, that was for sure.

Side by side they passed Baronsley's church, the next building to the restaurant. At the hotel, the sheriff paused.

'Let's see if Nelson Bush has heard anything about the shootin' last night,' he said.

'Who's Bush?' asked Matson.

'Owns the hotel. Big man. Fair-haired. Bit of a mystery. Bought the hotel mebbe twelve months ago. Spent a lot on it. Quiet. But allus packs a six-gun. Looks more like a range man than someone runnin' a hotel, but he seems to know what he's doin'.'

They pushed their way through the hotel doors. The clerk looked up. He scowled as he saw the visitors. Then his face blanked. He looked at Luke.

'Mornin', Mr Matson. Your room's been fixed.' He turned in his seat and produced a key.

A voice behind them said, 'Mornin',

Sheriff. Mornin', Mr Matson. My name's Bush — Nelson Bush. I was sorry to hear about the trouble last night. I'm glad to hear yuh want to stay here again tonight. Of course, there'll be no charge.'

The man fitted the sheriff's description. Late thirties or early forties. Wide-shouldered, slim, quietly dressed, tied-down Colt. But the eyes were the most noticeable feature — a light, hard blue, that seemed almost to question the frank smile on his face as he spoke.

'I'm obliged, Mr Bush,' Matson said. He told himself his thoughts were ridiculous. The worst thing you could say about the man — at first glance, too — was that he didn't look like a hotel owner.

But, in reply to Sheriff Stephens's questions, Bush could throw no light on the events of the previous night. He did, however, express no surprise at the appearance of Ingham and Rick Pallas on the scene just before the attempted shooting.

'Matthew Ingham's a regular customer,' he said, with a shrug that seemed to imply that he wasn't responsible for a man's reputation as long as he behaved himself in his hotel. 'In fact, Sheriff, he has a permanent room here, where he sometimes has a few friends in to play poker — that sort of thing.'

'Does he count Rick Pallas an' you among his friends, Mr Bush?' asked Matson.

Bush smiled, but Matson was studying those hard eyes. Either Bush was not bothered by the question or he was a good poker player. Matson fancied he could detect a slight undertone of annoyance in the hotelkeeper's voice when he answered, but told himself he was probably taking an instinctive dislike for someone too far. At his side, the sheriff seemed at ease with the man.

Bush said evenly, 'Mr Ingham's a valued and regular customer of the hotel, but I wouldn't call him a friend.' He looked straight at Matson and smiled. 'Any more than I reckon yuh'd call Rick Pallas a friend.'

'Seemed to me, when we met, the only friend he's likely to have is the Devil himself,' said Matson, returning the smile. Maybe, he thought, he'd been judging this man a little harshly. On the other hand, he could remember occasions when his first impressions of a man had helped to save his life.

From outside the hotel came the blast of a six-gun. Then another.

5

Luke Matson was at the sheriff's heels as they burst through the hotel's doors, closely followed by Nelson Bush. They could hear men shouting. Then, on the opposite side of the street, outside the entrance to the livery stable, the reason for the commotion became clear. Men huddled around a body lying sprawled face upwards in the dust. Sheriff Stephens pushed his way through the throng, Matson at his side. On the ground was the liveryman who had admired Matson's horse. But two bullet holes in the man's chest showed that his days of valuing good horseflesh were gone for ever.

Matson felt Nelson Bush thrust his way between him and Stephens. The hotel owner looked down at the body.

'Who in tarnation,' he asked, 'would want to shoot Pete Connors? It jest don't make sense. Pete wasn't interested in people. Hosses were his life. He knew more about them than any other man I ever met.' He looked at Matson. 'Any good hoss that found its way to his stable he tried to buy.'

The thought flashed through Matson's mind that for some reason Bush was fishing for information. But why? He would have guessed that Matson would leave his horse at the nearest livery stable. That wasn't important. And neither he nor the hotel owner could be implicated in the shooting — they were both with the sheriff when it happened. He decided to play along with Bush.

'He wanted mine as soon as I rode in,' said Matson. 'When I refused, that was that, he clammed up, almost seemed glad to see me go.' Not strictly true, but near enough for now.

For a moment he fancied he saw a slight sign of relief in the hard blue eyes. The only reason for that, he thought, would be that Bush wanted to know if he'd had any kind of a conversation with the liveryman. But that, too, didn't make much sense. Matson was a stranger, and what possible significance could a conversation between him and a liveryman have for the hotel owner?

His thoughts were broken into at that moment by the sheriff. 'Let's git the poor devil off the street,' he suggested. Together they moved the body into the stable. As they did so there came a whinny from the far end. There were half a dozen other horses there, but Matson recognized that sound at once.

'Quiet, boy,' he said, and whistled softly. There was silence.

Bush nodded his head. 'The black,' he said, 'he's yours?'

'He is,' said Matson. 'An' he's still not fer sale.'

'I can see why,' said Bush. At that, he turned away, nodded curtly to the sheriff, and left.

As he did so, the bulky figure of Matthew Ingham came through the stable doors from behind Matson.

Ingham wasted no time when he saw

the sheriff. 'They tell me Pete Connors's dead. Who killed him?'

Stephens indicated the body. 'You tell me,' he suggested.

Ingham scowled at him. 'One man dead, another badly wounded — both in the space o' twenty-four hours. You're the sheriff, ain't yuh?'

Matson saw the lawman's face turn rigid. But Stephens's voice was quiet. 'I was at the hotel with Luke here, an' Nelson Bush, when we heard the shots. Half the town must have heard, an' the way they were all millin' around would've given the killer an easy chance of a getaway.' His voice hardened. 'How come yuh didn't hear anything?'

'I was at the other end o' town,' snapped Ingham. He suddenly seemed to realize the implication of the sheriff's words. 'What the hell are yuh suggestin'?'

Stephens's voice was still cool, but there was a hard edge to it. 'I asked yuh a question. Yuh make what yuh like of it. Like yuh said, I'm the sheriff.' The hard edge deepened. 'An' I ask the questions. If yuh don't like it, what are yuh goin' to do about it?'

Luke Matson watched as the fat man fought to control his rage. He tried to speak, and failed. Finally, fists clenched, he snarled, turned on his heel, and pushed his way out again through the doors.

'Hell,' said Matson, drawing in his breath in a low whistle, 'I sure thought he was goin' to pull a gun on yuh.'

Stephens grinned at him. 'I reckon he will, some day,' he said. 'An' I jest hope I'm facin' him at the time.'

The two of them spent the next hour together as Stephens checked up on possible witnesses to the liveryman's death, but the lawman had little success. Nobody had seen anyone going into the stable. Nobody had seen the killer coming out after the killing. Everyone in the vicinity had heard the shots. A few had seen Connors crawl out of the stable doors and collapse. And that was all.

By the time the pair of them returned

to the office, Matson had formed an opinion of his own. One or two of the men questioned had hesitated, had seemed uneasy, or had been unable to look their questioner in the face. He looked at the sheriff, now sitting near him, mouth set in a straight line, fingers drumming on the table top.

'Some o' the fellers yuh were talkin' to seemed a bit close-mouthed somehow,' Matson said. 'Not at all like honest citizens used to co-operatin' with their local John Law.'

'Yuh noticed that, did yuh?' Stephens bent down, opened a drawer, and produced a bottle and glasses. He half-filled the glasses and pushed one across to Matson. 'I was thinkin' the same, an' it puzzled me. Ain't never had trouble in gittin' help when I've looked fer it, before today, anyway. I thought I must be mistaken, but if you, a stranger, noticed it, I guess I must have been right.' He shook his head, raised his glass, and drank deeply.

'Seemed to me,' said Matson, 'that it

weren't any reflection on yuh. One or two o' those fellers hesitated so long before answerin' your questions it looked as though they were scared to talk. As if the word had gone out — even before the shootin' — that it wouldn't be in anyone's interest to open his mouth if he'd seen anything.' He shook his head as the sheriff pushed the bottle towards him again. 'The girl last night, who was with Felix Wilson, what was her name?'

'Susan Tate. Her father, Andrew Tate, owns the Triangle T. A big spread jest a few miles north-east of here.' The sheriff poured whiskey into his own glass. 'What made yuh think of her jest now?'

Matson hesitated. Susan Tate had been emphatic in her belief that Rick Pallas had fired the shot which had almost killed Felix Wilson. What had made her so sure? And why had Wilson himself exonerated Pallas when his father had also suggested Pallas's name as the bushwhacker?

He shook his head. 'Somethin' an' nothin'. Both Susan Tate an' Felix Wilson's father were ready to blame Pallas fer the shootin' last night. But Felix himself said it wasn't Pallas. I jest had a thought. How did Felix know it wasn't?'

'Yuh mean Felix would never have got a look at him?'

'Guess so. It was dark, an' in any case, bushwhackers ain't in the habit o' showin' themselves if they can help it.'

'But you saw him,' said the sheriff. 'An' bluffed him. You've seen Pallas close up enough since then. Was it him?'

'I couldn't tell. The man was crouched down among the bushes. The only thing I was really sure of was the Winchester.'

The sheriff gazed reflectively into his now almost empty glass. He looked up finally. 'That makes two of us. Things have been happenin' in this town. An' I can't put a finger on any reason fer them.'

'What kind o' things?'

'I ain't sure. Yuh know, there's a hundred small towns like Baronsley. Cattlemen keep the town goin'. Tradesmen make a livin' from them — an' both sides more or less git along together. When any of 'em git out o' line, the law steps in to sort things out. An' compared with twenty years ago, when one man with enough *dinero* to hire a small army could whip a town into his own shape, it seems to work pretty well.'

Stephens twirled the empty glass in his hands, then put it down on the table. He shook his head. 'Over the last few months, there's been change. Townsfolk seem to be lookin' over their shoulders more, an' there's a tenseness in the air as if everyone's waitin' fer somethin' to happen. I don't like it.'

Matson said softly, 'Where does the killin' o' Connors, an' Felix Wilson's bushwhackin' fit in all this?'

'Nelson Bush was right,' said the sheriff. 'Didn't seem no reason fer

Connors to be killed. As fer Wilson, he an' Pallas don't like each other, but mostly they've kept out of each other's way, an' they ain't troubled me none.'

'An' Ingham?'

Stephens scowled. 'He's a mystery. He owns the Spanish Bull at the north end o' town. An' he reckons the livery stable is his, though I happen to know that it belonged to Pete Connors. Ingham doesn't know I know that. He an' Pallas spend a lot o' time together. Pallas don't seem to work, but he ain't ever short o' *dinero*.' The sheriff pushed his chair back and got to his feet.

Matson stretched and stood up. 'Seems to me yuh need cheerin' up,' he said. 'Let's go an' drown your sorrows in the Lucky Chance.'

The sheriff glanced wistfully at the half-empty bottle on the table.

'I'm buyin',' said Matson. He was now standing by the window, gazing out on to the street as he waited for the lawman. He watched idly as Rick Pallas came round the corner, heading in their direction. The gunman had almost reached the office when a figure stepped out of a nearby shop on the sidewalk.

It was Susan Tate.

Matson stiffened.

Pallas had deliberately turned and collided with the girl, and as she struggled to get away he clamped a hand roughly on her wrist and shook her. His face was livid. 'I want words with yuh, yuh troublemaker,' he yelled.

Susan Tate screamed angrily at him.

Matson leapt for the office door, swung it open, and cleared the five steps of the porch into the street. As he landed, he swept the forty-five from its holster.

6

'Pallas!' As Matson yelled the name, he chopped the forty-five across the man's arm muscles. Pallas stumbled to his knees and loosened his grip on the girl. Susan Tate, still looking dazed, stood still.

Matson slid the Colt back into its holster.

Rick Pallas climbed to his feet, swearing vividly. At the sight of Matson he went berserk. 'I'll kill yuh, *hombre*,' he snarled, and his arm flashed downwards.

But Luke Matson had already gone into action. His right hand moved in a blur of speed, catching his opponent full on the chin. As the gunman sagged, Matson sunk his left deep into the other's midriff. Pallas's eyes closed. He hit the ground and lay still.

Luke was conscious of Sheriff Stephens

standing by his side. The lawman looked at Susan Tate. 'You all right, Susan?' he demanded.

The girl looked back at him. The dazed look had vanished from her face. Suddenly, she smiled, a smile that encompassed both men. 'I'm fine now, Sheriff,' she said. 'Thanks to Mr Matson here.'

She held out a hand to Luke. He took it, and for a moment found himself face to face with her. She was, he had to acknowledge to himself, beautiful, and composed, despite her treatment by Pallas.

He said, almost apologetically, 'I'm glad I could help, Miss Tate. But it was nothin', really. Seein' him grab yuh jest riled me some.' He released her hand and stepped back.

As he did so, Pallas groaned, and tried to struggle to his feet.

The sheriff bent down and hauled him upright, none too gently. 'You were lucky. Had it been me, I wouldn't have used my fist. An' he only jest beat me to yuh.' His hand stretched out and yanked Pallas's Colt from its holster. 'There's a cell waitin' fer yuh.'

To Matson's surprise, Susan Tate put her hand on the lawman's arm. 'I'm not hurt, Sheriff. Let him go. Though I've no idea why he should have been so angry with me.'

Pallas scowled at her. 'I don't fergit in a hurry. Yuh said I shot that young Wilson you're walkin' out with. I had nothin' to do with it — but I reckon he had it comin', an' he's not the only one.'

Susan Tate's eyes opened wide. She looked startled. 'But how — ' She broke off, and turned away in confusion.

Luke Matson looked hard at the sheriff, a question forming on his lips. But the lawman almost imperceptibly shook his head.

Pallas said, with a sneer, 'Yuh heard her, Sheriff. Lemme go. Ain't nothin' yuh can do about it.' He looked hard at Matson. 'Keep out o' things that don't concern yuh, *hombre*. If'n you've got any sense you'll git out o' Baronsley, an' keep movin'.'

Stephens's dislike for the man showed deep in his eyes. He turned to Susan Tate, standing quietly by Luke Matson's side. He shook his head slowly. 'I sure hope yuh know what you're doin', Susan. Do yuh?'

Matson watched the girl's face whiten. But her voice was steady. 'Yes. Let him go, Sheriff. Please.'

The sheriff shrugged his shoulders. He released Pallas.

'I'll have my hawgleg, Stephens,' said the gunman with a scowl.

Matson watched as the sheriff stiffened, his face rigid with anger. Then the lawman visibly relaxed. He slowly ejected the slugs from Pallas's forty-five into the dust, and then tossed the weapon after them. 'There it is,' he said. 'Pick it up. Make one wrong move, an' I'll blow your head off.' He glared at the red-faced gunman and nodded at Susan Tate and Matson, 'Let's git out o' here,' he suggested. As they joined him, he turned his back on Pallas and moved contemptuously away, shepherding the other two into his office.

Once there, the sheriff sat facing them in silence, occasionally glancing in a puzzled way at the girl. Then he apparently made his mind up. 'What's goin' on, Susan?' he demanded abruptly.

She seemed to jump at the question, reddened, pulled herself together, and then shook her head. 'I don't know what you mean.'

To Matson's surprise, Stephens grinned at her. 'I don't much know what I mean either. But trouble's brewin'. Far as I can see, Felix Wilson an' his family an' you an' your father are on one side, while Ingham and Pallas figger prominently on the other.'

He leaned back in his chair and shook his head ruefully. 'Now what have we got? Felix Wilson is shot almost to death, an' Pete Connors, most of whose friends were hosses, is killed outside his livery stable, right in the centre o' town, in the middle o' the mornin'. Why?'

He got to his feet, strolled across to the window, and spent a few seconds gazing out into the street.

Luke Matson looked at the girl sitting quietly at his side. Then he noticed her hands. The knuckles were clenched tight, the fingers visibly shaking. He bent forward to speak to her.

But at that moment the sheriff rejoined them, sitting down again in his chair, and drumming his fingers on the table as he looked at them. He frowned, and shook his head. 'But it ain't nothin' to do with trouble between ranchers and townsfolk,' he said. 'I reckon there must have been near twenty or so folk who saw Pete Connors stumble, dyin', out o' the livery stable — an' someone must have seen his killer. Now, when I tried to make inquiries, half those I questioned seemed afraid to answer, an' the other half knew nothin'.' His face was grim. 'I ain't ever had that kind o' trouble before, in Baronsley.'

Susan Tate's voice was disturbed. 'You deserve better than that, Sheriff. But you're wrong about my father. I'm sure he knows nothing about this. As for me, I just happened to be there when Felix was shot.' She looked at Matson. 'I'd been spending the evening with Mrs Wilson — she hasn't been well lately — and Felix volunteered to see me home, as he generally did when I visited.' She paused, then she said, very softly, 'And Pallas was wrong. We are not walking out.'

The sheriff said gently, 'Why did yuh accuse Rick Pallas of bushwhackin' Felix?'

The colour rose in Susan Tate's cheeks. 'Mrs Wilson's worried half to death. She thinks Pallas is being hired to kill him. But she won't say why she thinks that. I tried to make her talk. I thought it would help her if only she could tell someone about it, but she won't.' She paused for a brief moment. 'When I saw Felix fall from his horse, I was frightened, and then I thought of Mrs Wilson — and her fears seemed to make sense, somehow. I don't like Pallas. I've seen what he's capable of, and I honestly thought he must have shot Felix.'

She stood up, her face sober. 'I'm sorry, Sheriff, but I can't tell you anything more.'

The sheriff opened the door for her. 'You've helped more than yuh know, Susan.'

She smiled at him. And then she looked at Luke Matson, now standing by the table. Once more she smiled. 'Goodbye, Mr Matson. And thank you for your timely help once again.'

Both Matson and the sheriff were silent after Susan Tate had left. Since his wife's death no woman had featured in Matson's life, and he suddenly realized that a fact that had for ten years seemed right, and even comforting, had in the last few minutes become less than essential when confronted with the warmth of this woman's smile.

Angrily, he mentally accused himself of being false to the memory of the dead. But then a new thought struck him. Pallas had said Felix Wilson was walking out with Susan Tate. Just now, however, Susan had denied this. To add to his confusion, the thought cheered him.

But Sheriff Stephens, sitting quietly at his side, looked at him and rose from his chair. 'She's a nice girl, Susan,' he said. 'I'm thinkin' o' takin' a stroll round town. Talk to a few more folk. Try to git some idea o' what's happenin', an' why. Comin'?'

Glad to put his somewhat disjointed thoughts behind him for a while, Matson found himself outside in the street with the lawman. For an hour they talked with townsfolk. Most, though they had heard the shots, had been too far away at the time to be of any help. As before, one or two had been on the spot but swore that they had seen no one. A few even managed to look uneasy, but shook their heads when asked direct questions. Only a general picture emerged: two shots had been fired; Pete Connors, clutching his chest, hands covered in blood, had crawled from the livery stable and collapsed, dying, in the street outside. He had mumbled something, but nobody knew what.

Finally, the sheriff and Luke Matson went back to the livery stable. Here again, a thorough search revealed nothing but that the killer must have entered the stable through a back door which led to the small room which had been Connors's living quarters, and from which another door opened into the stable itself.

Just before they left, Matson stopped at a stall.

'He's a lovely animal,' said Stephens admiringly, at the sight of the black's greeting to Matson.

Matson nodded in agreement. But his attention was focused on the back of the horse's stall. There, someone had left a message. Or part of one. Scrawled in red. Not, he realized, in ink or paint. There had been no time for that.

The sheriff looked puzzled. 'What's wrong, Luke?'

'Look at this.' Matson waved an arm towards the back of the stall.

Stephens joined him. He, too, looked hard at the shaky letters: TELL JB WHERE W — . A streak of blood stretched from the final letter to the floor.

Matson said, 'Mean anything to yuh?'

The sheriff shook his head. 'Nope. But it must have meant a whole heap to poor Pete Connors. Two holes in his chest an' he still finds the strength to try an' leave a message — in blood. Halfway through, he falls down, can't git up again, and finally, on his hands and knees, reaches the street. It sure must have been important to him.' He turned away. 'Hell, another few seconds an' he might have finished it. He deserved that, poor devil.'

He stood up. His eyes were bleak. 'I'm goin' to find out, if it costs me my star. But I'll need help.' For a second the bleakness left his face as he looked at his companion.

Luke Matson said simply, 'I'll be around.'

7

'What d'yuh reckon?' Stephens handed Luke Matson a slip of paper on which was copied the cryptic message from the livery-stable wall.

Matson studied it closely and then nodded. 'It ain't much to go on,' he said. 'But it might jest jog someone's memory.'

The sheriff pushed away his office chair and reached for his Stetson. 'Let's yuh an' me go an' find this *hombre*,' he suggested.

'Where d'yuh reckon to try first?' Matson joined him outside.

The lawman gave him a pitying look. 'Where most of Baronsley'll be found at this time,' he said.

They were outside the Lucky Chance before Stephens spoke again. 'Here we are. Let's give Bud Jenning the first chance.' He pushed through the batwing doors.

The bar-room was almost full. Stephens stood watching the scene, and as Matson joined him the lawman grinned at him. 'There's a dozen ol'-timers in that crowd. One of 'em must be able to help us,' he said. 'Ain't nowhere else you'd find 'em all together.'

'You're gittin' too cocky in your old age,' said Matson. 'I reckon no one here can help yuh. Loser buys the drinks.'

They reached the bar. A sweating Bud Jenning looked up at them. Stephens pushed the piece of paper under his nose.

'I ain't got no time fer playin' games.' The barkeep scowled. 'That mob out there must've spent the last six months in a desert.' He looked hard at the sheriff. 'All the talk's about the killin' o' Pete Connors an' Felix Wilson's bushwhackin'.' He dropped his voice. 'Earlier on this evenin' a couple of fellers were mighty free with their likker, an' then they got to suggestin' that the sheriff of Baronsley either weren't up to his job, or he was in cahoots with the killers.' He looked at Matson. 'They also want to know why some stranger who was supposed to be unarmed when Wilson was attacked, was carryin' a hawgleg a few hours later.' He broke off, produced a bottle and glasses, put them down in front of Stephens, and hurried down to the far end of the bar.

Stephens poured the drinks. 'Yuh don't have to be involved in this, yuh know, Luke. Yuh want to ride on, I'll understand.'

'What'll they say then, Sheriff?' Matson grinned at him. 'Besides, I'm beginnin' to like the place — especially when you're buyin'.'

'Someone, today, is goin' to work out the message on this here paper,' said the sheriff. 'Then we'll see who's buyin'.'

Bud Jenning rejoined them. Not looking at them, he said, 'Ingham an' Pallas.'

Stephens shook his head sadly. 'They

won't buy us a drink, Bud.'

The barkeep shook his head just as sadly. 'It's the drink,' he said mournfully. 'I knew it'd git him, sooner or later. Let it be a lesson to yuh, Mr Matson. You're headin' down the same road to destruction.'

'Before I git plumb out o' sight on that road,' said Matson, 'supposin' yuh join me in one last drink.'

Bud Jenning mopped his brow. 'It's hot in here tonight,' he said. 'Mighty hot. Mebbe I will join yuh — jest this once, to ease this ragin' thirst. But don't git any ideas. I ain't goin' to enjoy it.'

He splashed whiskey into a glass and raised it to his lips. The level of the drink dropped like a stone.

'While yuh ain't enjoyin' that drink,' said the sheriff, putting the slip of paper on the bar once again, 'jest pass your whiskey-sodden ol' eyes over this here message, will yuh?'

The barkeep stared hard at the paper, then he said slowly, ' "Tell JB where W . . . ' Don't make sense nohow. No sir.' He scratched his chin. 'Who in tarnation is 'JB'?'

And that question seemed to be asked in turn by everyone in the bar when Sheriff Stephens produced the message.

Only one old-timer seemed to show a spark of recognition. 'JB, JB,' he muttered into his empty glass. 'Hell, Sheriff, guess my throat's too dry to think straight.'

The sheriff tilted the bottle he was carrying. The old man swallowed gratefully, 'That's better. Now, lemme see. JB? Yep. It's comin' back to me.' He waved his glass hopefully. Stephens bent his arm once more. The old-timer drank, smacked his lips and half-closed his eyes. 'That's right. JB. Joshua Brighton. Went to Shotley 'bout ten years ago.' He leaned back in his chair and finished his drink.

The lawman gazed triumphantly at Luke Matson. 'Looks like you're payin'', Luke,' he said. 'I'll telegraph Shotley in the mornin'.' He patted the old-timer on the shoulder. 'Billy Welch, I'm sure obliged to yuh. D'yuh reckon this Brighton could still be there?'

The old man's face split into a huge grin. 'At Shotley? I'm durn sure he is, Sheriff. He didn't want to go, but they dragged him there, an' hung him fer hoss-stealin'. He's still there — on Boot Hill.'

A yell of delight went up from the tables around them.

Matson looked at Stephens's face and waited for the explosion. To his surprise, the sheriff stood stock-still for a full minute. Then his mouth twitched. He put a hand over his eyes, and his shoulders shook in a fever of wild laughter. He slowly recovered, and turned to the old-timer, who sat motionless in his chair, his face white as chalk.

Stephens grinned at the old man. 'Billy, I walked into that like a durned pilgrim,' he admitted ruefully. He placed the bottle of whiskey on the table at the oldster's elbow. 'It's yours — you've earned it.'

He turned and looked at the still laughing crowd. 'You've had your fun, an' I enjoyed it too. But what's written on this paper are the words Pete Connors scrawled on the wall of the livery stable in his own blood. Then he crawled into the street to die. I'd like to find out what he was tryin' to tell us — I reckon he deserves as much.'

He walked to the bar, followed by a crowd. He put the slip of paper on the bar top. 'I'd be obliged if all of yuh would have a look at this, an' if it means anything to anyone mebbe he'll let me know.'

At his side, Matson said softly, 'I'm buyin'.' He managed to catch the barkeep's attention. A bottle was slid to him and three glasses. For a moment he wondered about the extra glass, but when he turned round Stephens was no longer there. Then an arm was raised at a table at the far end of the counter. It was the lawman, with a stranger, a man looking to be in his late forties, heavily built, hair still dark. He nodded in a friendly manner as Matson joined them.

The sheriff said, 'Luke, this is Andrew Tate, Susan's father.'

Tate's handshake was firm. 'Mr Matson,' he said, 'I've been lookin' forward to meetin' yuh. My daughter reckons if yuh hadn't been there Felix Wilson wouldn't be alive today, an yuh also came to her aid when Pallas tried to threaten her. We're in your debt, Mr Matson.'

Matson nodded. 'Glad to be able to help, Mr Tate,' he said, filling the glasses as he spoke. 'An' Pallas an' me had already had a run-in once before — here. Seems he don't take kindly to strangers.'

'I would've taken bets that he bushwhacked Felix,' said Tate. 'But Wilson himself told my daughter that it wasn't Pallas.'

Matson looked at the sheriff. 'I knew I'd overlooked somethin'. Pallas reckoned

81

she'd accused him o' shootin' young Wilson. But that night, when I arrived, she was bendin' over Wilson an' didn't look up. She thought I was the bushwhacker an' she said, 'You've killed him, Pallas. What are yuh goin' to do now — kill me?' Now, I was there, she was there, an' mebbe the bushwhacker was still there — in hidin'. But no one else was there. So, either Pallas did the shootin' or the bushwhacker told him what Susan had said. That means, if Pallas didn't fire the shot, he sure knows who did.'

The sheriff said quietly, 'Luke reckons that, when the bushwhacker came back, all he could see was a figure crouchin' in the bushes. At that time he hadn't met Pallas, an' even now he can't tell who the bushwhacker was. So, why was Felix so certain that it wasn't Pallas, when it ain't likely that he ever saw who fired the shot?'

Tate turned to the sheriff. 'Why not ask Felix himself?' he said. 'Tell yuh what, I'm goin' out to the Bar W myself this afternoon with Susan, jest to see how Felix is makin' out. Why don't yuh come too? That way yuh can git any information yuh want without makin' it look like official business.' He looked at Luke and smiled. 'I hope you'll come as well, Mr Matson. We'll be glad to have yuh along.'

For a moment Luke Matson had a vision of Susan Tate as he had seen her at the Wilson ranch, sitting quietly by the fire, her voice soft and warm and friendly. He hesitated. But the thought of meeting Andrew Tate's daughter again was a pleasant one. He said, 'I'd like that, Mr Tate. I'd like that very much.'

As he spoke, he was conscious of the sheriff's eyes on him — a look somewhere between a smile and a question.

But all the sheriff said was, 'That goes fer me too, Andrew. In the meantime, Luke an' me are goin' to visit the Bull. We'll see if anyone there can make sense o' Pete Connors's message.' He turned to Matson. 'Fer Gawd's sake don't let Bud Jenning know you've been there.'

'What message are yuh talkin' about?' Andrew Tate leaned forward in his seat, his face showing interest.

Stephens pointed to the bar, where a small knot of customers were clustered around his note. 'Yuh weren't here when we came in,' he said. He put down his empty glass. 'Let's have a look now.'

Together, he and the rancher pushed their way through to the bar. Matson watched as the two men reached it. But then he saw Tate's shake of the head as the sheriff showed him the message.

★   ★   ★

As he and the sheriff walked into the bar of the Spanish Bull, Matson became instantly aware of a sudden change in the atmosphere. Men swung round in their seats, scowling at the sight of the newcomers. The bartender put down the glasses he was polishing and deliberately turned his back as Matson and the sheriff reached him.

There was a long pause. Matson watched as the sheriff stood silent, his face expressionless. The large, badly lit room showed signs of neglect. The bar-length mirror had fought a losing battle with flies and nicotine, and the low ceiling bore witness to drunken customers' prowess with six-guns.

His thoughts were interrupted by the action of the lawman.

Stephens's voice was low and even, and icy. 'This barkeep's name is Smith,' he informed Matson. 'An' he's fixin' to show his pardners here jest how tough he is. But I'm bettin' I can make him turn an' serve us before yuh can count five. What d'yuh say?'

Matson swung round, his back to the bar, right hand hanging loose. 'Nope,' he said. 'I ain't bettin'. An' I ain't lookin' either. I can't abide the sight o' blood. Especially barkeep's. It ain't like an ordinary *hombre*'s somehow. The likker seems to turn the colour yellow.' He was studying the room as he spoke, but he sensed an increase in the tension as the barkeep turned to face the sheriff.

Half a dozen men seemed to stiffen in their seats at the movement. Two of them, sitting a few feet from where he was standing, scowled and half rose. Matson turned slightly so that he was directly facing them. His hand moved a few inches towards his holster.

He nodded amiably at the men. 'Yuh two. Jest sit comfortable now. If your pardners decide to take a hand here, I reckon I could git yuh both before they moved.'

The pair froze in their seats.

Out of the corner of his eye Matson saw the barkeep's hand move stealthily under the bar counter. Then the man screamed as the barrel of a six-gun smashed across his wrist. Matson heard the sheriff's voice and grinned to himself at the quiet tone.

'It's jest possible yuh weren't a

hankerin' to grab that scatter-gun you've got under there, so I'm givin' yuh the benefit of a sizeable doubt — providin' yuh can put a couple o' glasses o' your rotgut on the counter with your good hand. My friend an' me are a mite thirsty.'

A bottle and two glasses appeared as if by magic.

Stephens passed a glass to Matson, who ostensibly took it in his left hand. Sullen faces in the crowd watched in an unfriendly silence. Then as Matson raised his glass to his mouth the batwing doors at the far end of the room swung open.

At his side, the sheriff whistled softly. 'What d'yuh reckon to those two for strange bedfellows?'

Matthew Ingham and Nelson Bush stood side by side in the entrance.

Ingham's face purpled at the sight of the two figures at the bar. He pushed his way through to them, followed by Bush. The fat man swore at the barkeep. 'What in tarnation are yuh doin', Smith? I told yuh yesterday these two are not to be served in here.'

Before the white-faced barkeep could speak, the sheriff stepped between him and Ingham. 'Let's git a couple o' things straight, Ingham,' he said. 'I'm in here on official business. An' if I wasn't, an' your barkeep refuses to serve me or anyone with me, I'll close this place down. It won't be hard to find a reason.'

Ingham sneered. 'What official business, Stephens?'

The lawman produced the note and thrust it under the fat man's nose. 'It's a copy o' Pete Connors's last words,' he gritted. 'Written in his own blood on the livery-stable wall. Look at it, Ingham. I'm still askin' the questions. I'm stayin' here till everyone in this room has read it. You're first.'

Hands clenched, Ingham snatched the note from him and slowly read it, with Nelson Bush peering over his shoulder. Face still blank, the fat man handed the note back to the sheriff.

'Don't mean a damn thing to me,' he muttered.

But Matson had been watching Nelson Bush and had seen the look of apprehension, almost dread, that had suddenly flickered in the hotel-owner's hard blue eyes.

8

The sun was still high in the sky when Luke Matson and the sheriff met Andrew Tate and his daughter outside the hotel and rode out of town. Two miles from Baronsley the trail split in two. Tate waved an arm towards the right-hand fork.

'The Triangle T ranch-house is three miles over there, jest through that stand o' cottonwoods,' he said to Matson. 'We'll be glad to see yuh any time.'

Matson nodded his thanks. He glanced across to where Susan Tate sat on her horse. There was a warmth in her smile.

'Do come and see us, Mr Matson. Dad is right. You'll be welcome any time.'

At that moment the sheriff reined in his horse. 'Something's wrong,' he said. 'Someone's in a hell of a hurry.'

Five hundred yards away a horse and

rider exploded into view around a corner. At the sight of the rancher, a voice yelled an urgent message, lost in the drumming of hoofbeats.

Andrew Tate looked astonished. 'It's Martha Wilson. Hell, I've never seen her ride a horse like that.' He spurred his own mount to meet the frantic woman, reaching up and steadying her horse as it skidded to a halt in a cloud of dust.

The woman, eyes staring, mouth working convulsively, clung to him. 'It's John, it's John,' she managed to get out. 'First Felix, now John. Why can't they leave us alone? He came home an hour ago . . . He fell out of the saddle . . . He's been shot in the back . . . He's dying, dying.' She shook her head, sorrow stark in her face. 'I'm going to fetch Doc Parkinson. Janet is looking after her father while I'm gone.'

Tate said, gently, 'Sheriff Stephens'll take yuh back home, Martha. I'll fetch the doctor.' He wheeled his mount and was gone.

By the time they reached the Wilson spread, Susan had managed to calm the distraught woman a little. But then, Matson and the sheriff watched as Tate's daughter, half-led, half-carried her now-weeping companion up the steps of the ranch-house's porch. The door opened and a slim figure ran to the top of the steps.

'That's Janet,' said the sheriff. 'If her father is as bad hit as Martha says, that girl is goin' to be hurt worst of all.'

Matson followed the sheriff into the house. When they reached the living-room the three women had vanished. As they sat down they heard footsteps on the stairs. Susan Tate came back into the room.

Matson stood up and pulled a chair into place for her. 'How is he?'

She shook her head. 'Still unconscious. Janet's doing her best to cope, but Martha still doesn't seem to know what's going on. Poor woman. First Felix, now her husband. It must be terrible for her.'

The sheriff said, 'In all the confusion

I'd forgotten it was Felix we came to see. Any news of him?'

'He's mending slowly. But he's still not allowed any visitors.' She was silent for a moment, then she said, 'I'm going to make some coffee. Could you and Luke go upstairs and persuade Martha and Janet to come down and have some while you look after John?'

Matson led the way upstairs and into the bedroom. The two pale-faced women looked up at them as they bent over the rancher. He lay motionless, eyes closed, features drained of colour. Martha Wilson clutched the sheriff's arm. 'Is he . . . ? Is he . . . ?'

It was Matson who stooped low over the prostrate man. He put three fingers on his wrist. At first there was nothing. No movement. Then the feeblest of motions — a faint glimmer of a pulse.

Luke whispered, 'He's alive. He's goin' to make it.'

The girl was holding her mother tight. 'You hear that? You hear that?' she entreated.

Martha Wilson's body was shaking, tears streaming down her ravaged face. 'I thought he was dead. Dear God, I was sure he was dead.'

'Let him rest quietly,' suggested Matson. 'The doctor'll be here any time now. You an' Janet go on down. Susan's makin' coffee. The sheriff an' me'll stay here fer a while.'

Janet Wilson put a comforting arm around her still-dazed mother and led her to the door. There she stopped and faced Matson, a question manifest in her eyes. He looked at her, smiled, and nodded. The bleak look slowly faded from her young face. She turned and, now hand in hand with her mother, disappeared down the stairs.

Stephens breathed out noisily. He gave Matson a searching look.

'He's breathin',' said Matson. 'Now it all depends on the doctor.'

He had hardly spoken when a door swung open and there was the sound of hurried footsteps on the stairs. The next moment Andrew Tate was in the

94

bedroom, followed by the doctor. There was silence as he bent over the unconscious man. At last he straightened up. His face was serious.

'I reckon you called me just in time,' he said. He looked across to where Stephens stood. 'Two gunshot victims in the same family, Sheriff. What's going on in Baronsley?'

The sheriff shook his head. 'At the moment your guess is as good as mine,' he admitted. 'I'd hoped to have a few words with Felix today. But I hear he's not fit enough yet to answer questions.'

'Give him another two or three days,' said the doctor. He looked down at the motionless figure on the bed. 'And as for John here, it could be weeks before he can answer questions, if not longer.'

Matson had a picture in his mind of Martha Wilson sobbing out the question, 'Why can't they leave us alone?' Did she have any idea who 'they' were?

His thoughts were disturbed.

Doc Parkinson came away from the bedside. 'Yes, John's a strong man,' he said. 'He should pull through, but he must not be moved or worried in any way.' He picked up his bag. 'Let's go down. He'll sleep for hours now. And I'll have a look at Felix while I'm here.'

It was quiet in the living-room. Martha Wilson and her daughter sat, heads bowed, at the table, with Susan Tate standing behind them. The three looked up as the men came into the room.

Martha Wilson got to her feet. She tried to speak but failed. Then she managed to whisper, 'He's going to die, isn't he?'

Matson heard her daughter's half-strangled sob at the question.

But the doctor gently pushed the older woman back into her chair. 'Martha,' he said, 'your husband is a very sick man. But he's going to get better — and so is your son. It'll be a long job and a hard one, but with you and Janet helping, it'll come right in the end.'

Susan Tate said, 'What can we do to help?'

Doc Parkinson smiled at her. 'Could you possibly stay, Susan? John and Felix will not wake, I promise you. But Martha and Janet have been through a terrible ordeal. If you could persuade them to go to bed and stay there till as late as possible tomorrow morning, that'll be better than any medicine I could give them.'

That would mean three women and two helpless men left in the ranch-house, thought Matson. What if a bushwhacker took a notion to come and finish the job? He opened his mouth to speak, but was interrupted.

Andrew Tate said, 'That's a good idea, Susan. I'll stay as well.'

The sheriff looked at Susan and then at Matson. 'I must git back,' he said. 'Two bushwhackings, an' a killin', already. If I ain't in Baronsley tomorrow to try an' pick up some sort o' trail, there'll be hell to pay.'

He turned to Matson. 'But you stay, Luke.'

'I'd be glad to help,' said Matson. 'If Mr Tate an' his daughter have no objection.'

Stephens looked at the rancher. Tate said, 'Luke, I'm obliged.'

Susan Tate lifted her head and said warmly, 'You seem to make a habit of being around when needed, Luke. Thank you.'

As the sheriff got up, the doctor stopped him. 'Before you go, Sheriff, what's this about a message Pete Connors left before he died?'

'That?' Stephens fumbled in a pocket. 'I got a copy somewhere.' He handed a crumpled piece of paper to the doctor.

'Tell JB where W . . . ' The doctor read the words aloud. 'Doesn't make sense, Sheriff.'

At once, Martha Wilson was on her feet, wide-eyed, gasping. 'Let me see that! I must see that!'

Susan Tate, white-faced, clutched her

arm. 'No Martha! No!'

But the woman pushed her aside and snatched the note from the doctor. Colour drained from her face as she read it. 'Oh no,' she muttered. She turned away, buckled at the knees and collapsed.

9

In the evening, Luke Matson watched as the sheriff mounted his horse and left for Baronsley, before leaving the ranch-house himself. A few minutes later he shifted his position in the corner of a barn and waited, ears tuned to the slight noise which had disturbed him. He moved soundlessly to the door. From there he could see the nearby ranch-house outlined against the faint moonlight. The sound came again, now recognizable as soft footsteps moving in his direction. Puzzled, but still wary, he melted into the shadows.

Then a figure appeared in the doorway. A soft voice whispered, 'Luke, are you there?'

It was Susan Tate. He moved to join her. He could now make out her features, but her smile faded when he asked, 'How's Mrs Wilson?'

She sighed. 'She's sleeping now, but she's very disturbed.'

'Not surprisin'. Husband an' son both shot near to death.'

She looked up at him, and hesitated for a moment. Then she said, 'Luke, Felix isn't Martha Wilson's son.'

He said, 'No. But the Wilsons adopted him, didn't they? That's what I hear.' He waited. The strengthening moon showed the passage of conflicting emotions across Susan's features.

'It shouldn't be me telling you this,' she said, entwining her hands nervously. 'But Martha can't, and I convinced her you could help.' Her face coloured, but her eyes were steady. 'Martha's living a nightmare. She had given me hints before, but tonight she told me the whole story.'

He looked at her troubled face and took her hands in his. She did not take them away.

'Martha's sister, Helen, was Felix's mother. She died not long after he was born. Martha and John adopted him.

That's the easy part.'

He could feel both her closeness and the sadness in her voice. 'An' what's the hard part?' he said gently.

'Helen's husband had a ranch two hundred miles south of here, Makensville way. She was his second wife. He swore the baby was not his and threw them both out. Martha told me his son from his previous marriage had gone to the bad, and that might have soured him.'

'Where's that son now?'

'No one knows. He was fifteen when he ran away from home — shortly after his mother died. A year later Helen married his father. Martha has heard nothing of them since Helen died. That's more than twenty years ago. Felix is twenty-two, and his half-brother must be in his late thirties.'

Luke was puzzled. He couldn't see any connection between the shootings and Martha's story. And anyway, Susan's nearness was making it difficult to concentrate on anything else. In the moonlight she stood straight and still, looking into his eyes, now smiling at the look on his face as he remained silent.

'What is it, Luke?' she asked quietly.

He put his arms around her and held her close, still saying nothing.

She said, so softly that he had to bend his head to hear, and with her lips almost touching his, 'It's not just the moonlight, is it, Luke?'

He kissed her, holding her face between his hands, and looking deep into her eyes. 'No, it's not just the moonlight, Susan. It's for night and day, day and night, as long as I live.'

She sighed then and reached up and kissed him. 'I'm glad, Luke, so glad.'

What seemed a long time later, he said, 'I sure don't want to git back to other people's troubles, but I still can't see why Mrs Wilson thinks I can help her. Yuh haven't told me anything that links anyone with the shootings.'

She turned within the circle of his arms and then back again to face him. 'It was the note. I'm sure that's why Martha was so upset. She told me that

Felix's father's name was Barton. James Barton. 'J.B.' It fits the note. But I've no idea who the 'W' is.'

'I can understand her worryin' about it,' he said. 'But it could just be a coincidence. And the fact that two of Martha's family were bushwhacked round about the same time that Pete Connors was killed doesn't mean the three things are connected.'

'And the 'W'? What could that mean?'

He shook his head. 'Only Pete Connors knew what that meant. But it must have been important fer a dyin' man to try so hard to git a message through.' He looked at her. 'Let's hope the sheriff can work somethin' out in the next few days. He's a good lawman, an' he's gittin' real mad at Ingham an' Pallas fer the lies they've been spreadin'.'

She said quietly, 'And you, Luke. What do you think about Ingham and Pallas? And the sheriff?'

'Ingham's mixed up in this some-where. He hates the sheriff, but that's purely personal. Pallas, on the other hand, is jest a tough gunfighter, used fer any dirty work that's needed.'

It was then that he heard the noise. Not a night animal. The slight scrape of a boot heel, or the softer sound perhaps of leather on wood as someone brushed against the side of the barn.

He whispered to Susan, 'We've got a visitor. Move back out of line with the door, while I find out what's goin' on.'

Cautiously he moved along the wall, almost to the door. He stood in a pool of shadow, his forty-five in his hand. There was no sound.

Inch by inch he moved until he finally reached the door. The moon was now hidden, the ranch-house a grey shape in the gloom. He froze. A darker shape in the grey was moving stealthily towards the house.

He waited.

Then from a distance came a whistle. Repeated twice. The shape seemed to melt into the darkness.

He waited again. He had to strain to

hear the quiet footsteps until they finally faded away. At last came the distant sound of hoofbeats.

He called softly, 'Susan.'

Almost immediately she was at his side.

'Wait,' he said. He stood outside the barn door, but there was no further sound, not even the sighing of the night wind.

He took the girl's arm. 'Back to the house,' he said.

At the door she turned to him. 'What are you going to do, Luke?'

'I'll stick around,' he said. 'I could pick out the sound of two horses movin' out. The whistle must have been a signal to the other *hombre*. I don't think they'll be back. You go in now, an' try to git some sleep.' He put his arms around her and kissed her.

She smiled happily up at him and put a finger to his lips. 'Take care, Luke,' she said softly. Then she was gone.

★　★　★

The first pale rays of the morning sun brought a touch of comfort into Matson's stiff limbs as he stood up in the corner of the porch where he had spent the last hour of his vigil. He looked out over the Bar W range at the stand of cottonwoods, split by the fork between the ranch and the Baronsley trail. He nodded quietly to himself at a sudden thought, and strolled over to the corral. The black whinnied contentedly and came to his side.

Five minutes later he was riding round the edge of the stand. He reached a lone tree near the fork and turned in towards it.

He dismounted. There were two sets of hoof marks, and the footprints of one man, near a thicket. He found where the man had remounted, and followed the tracks until they merged with others at the fork. It was clear that the previous night one man had stayed with the horses, while another had made his way to the ranch-house. What was not clear was why the intruder's visit had been cut short by the man with the horses whistling a warning.

He remounted, and sat still, head bowed.

The answer came to him. Two men had seen him, the sheriff, and Andrew Tate arrive at the ranch. But later the watcher in the trees had realized that only the sheriff had left the house, leaving Tate and him on guard, and had called back his companion.

Matson whistled softly to himself. If Andrew Tate had not suggested a visit to the Bar W the previous afternoon, somebody could well have finished the job of killing both Felix Wilson and his father.

He turned his horse and headed back to the ranch.

10

As they sat having breakfast in the kitchen of the Bar W, Andrew Tate glanced across to where his daughter sat next to Luke Matson. There was a puzzled look on the rancher's face. Susan smiled at him.

He said, 'You're lookin' mighty pleased with yourself this mornin'.'

'It's a lovely morning, Dad,' she said demurely.

He said nothing for a moment. Then he shook his head. 'It was a lovely mornin' yesterday. An' come to think of it, so it was the mornin' before, an' the mornin' before that.' He looked hard at her companion. 'What d'yuh think, Luke?'

Luke Matson grinned at the older man. 'I'd have to agree with Susan,' he said. 'Fer me this is the finest mornin' in many a long year.'

The rancher stared open-mouthed at the pair of them. Colour flooded his face. Then he laughed out loud. 'Well, I'll be durned. So that's the way of it.'

At that moment the kitchen door opened and Janet Wilson came in. The two men got to their feet. Luke could see the suffering in her face as she sat down. But it was Andrew Tate who spoke first.

'Janet, how are Felix an' John?'

The girl was slow to answer. Her eyes were red-rimmed and her face grey with fatigue. Finally, she said, 'They slept through. They're still asleep, thank heavens. Mother had a bad night, and I'm not going to wake her yet.'

Susan had gone through into the kitchen. Now she returned with a tray of food and a mug of coffee.

'Have your breakfast,' she said to the girl. 'And then you're going to get some rest yourself. Don't worry, I'll look after your mother. I'll be staying all day.'

Andrew Tate said, 'In that case I reckon Luke an' me'll have a look outside to see what wants doin'.'

Luke was behind the rancher as he reached the porch. In the morning light the range, stretching to the mist-shrouded distant hills, seemed peaceful and serene.

Tate followed his gaze. 'Quiet, ain't it, Luke?'

'It was quiet last night,' said Matson. 'An' there were a couple of *hombres* staked out in those cottonwoods. One of 'em made his way here, but the other one signalled to him, an' he went back to the trees.'

'What made him go back?'

'I reckon his pardner saw the sheriff leave on his own an' realized two of us had stayed behind, an' he didn't fancy the odds.'

'The one who came here. Did yuh see him?'

Matson shrugged. 'Nope. He never came out of the shadows. I could have plugged him, but that wouldn't have answered any questions. It would jest have woken the house.'

Tate said, 'Yuh did right, Luke. They expected to find jest two women an' a couple o' badly wounded men. They slunk away like coyotes.' He scowled. 'Mostly John an' Felix work this spread on their own — with Janet helpin' when necessary. She rates as a tophand in my book, jest like Susan. But now . . . ' He shook his head and lapsed into silence.

Luke Matson watched as varying emotions passed swiftly across the man's weatherbeaten face, but said nothing.

The rancher looked up at last. 'Hell, everyone around here seems to need help. Even the sheriff. He's a good man an' we don't want to lose him.' He stopped.

Matson fixed his eyes on the hills in the distance. His voice was quiet. 'I know. I sorta agreed to stick around fer a while.'

Relief appeared in Tate's eyes. 'I thought so. Now, I'll bring help from the Triangle. That'll keep things goin' here, an' then yuh can go back to town.'

He smiled suddenly. 'Susan'll miss yuh, but the sooner you an' Stephens sort this business out, the sooner things can git back to normal. In any case, yuh come out here or to the Triangle whenever yuh git the chance. We'll both be glad to see yuh.'

*   *   *

The noonday sun was blazing down relentlessly when Luke Matson rode into Baronsley. As he reached the sheriff's office, Stephens himself appeared. He stopped short as he saw Matson.

Matson explained what had happened, and how, as a result, Andrew Tate had brought three of his men back to the Bar W. They were to take over the running of the ranch and guard it night and day until they were no longer needed, whenever that might be.

The sheriff nodded in satisfaction. 'Tate's a good neighbour,' he acknowledged. He made his way back into the office. Once inside, he sat down heavily in a chair, and drummed his fingers moodily on the table. 'I'm baffled, Luke. Nothin' seems to make sense. I got this feelin' that sooner or later all hell's goin' to be let loose — an' I ain't goin' to be able to stop it.' He shook his head and then fished a bottle out of a drawer. He splashed whiskey into two glasses.

Matson accepted the proffered drink and leaned back in his chair. He looked at the older man. 'Did yuh know Martha Wilson had a sister?'

The sheriff shook his head.

Matson said, 'Her name was Helen. She was a rancher's wife. They lived near Makensville. She had a baby, a son. Now, listen to this. Her husband, who had been married before, threw her out. She came to live with the Wilsons, but died soon after.' He stopped and looked across the table at the sheriff.

Stephens picked up his glass. He drank and put it down again. He said slowly, 'This would all have happened before I came here. Let me guess. The Wilsons brought the boy up as their own. End of story.'

'You're right. Felix Wilson is John and Martha's adopted son. But there's more.'

The sheriff put his glass down carefully. His eyes were fixed on his companion.

'Helen's husband had a son from his first marriage. When he was fifteen the boy ran away from home — jest after his mother died. It was twelve months later that Helen married his father.'

The lawman still looked puzzled. 'So?'

Matson paused before answering. Then he said, 'Helen's husband's name was Barton — James Barton.'

The sheriff looked at him. 'This Barton. Is he still alive?'

'Martha didn't say. But one thing was for sure. He was no small-time rancher. He had one of the biggest spreads fer miles around. But he wasn't a happy man. One son had disappeared, and he had disowned the other. His first wife had died, and the talk was that the second, Helen, was almost killed by neglect before he finally threw her out.'

The sheriff said, 'Pete Connors's message was simple — pity no one can understand it. 'Tell JB where W — .' Who's 'W'? Couldn't be Wilson, could it?'

Matson shook his head. 'Not likely. Barton would know where the Wilsons were livin'. What's more important, my friend, is, where does 'W' fit in? For instance, Connors could have meant, where 'W' is; or was; or was goin' to be.'

Stephens picked up his glass and drained it. 'Let's suppose Connors intended to write, 'Tell JB where W is.' What then?'

'That would mean that Connors not only knew JB. He also knew this feller, 'W'. An', probably most of all, he knew how important it was to let JB know 'W's' whereabouts. So, he spent his last seconds tryin' to git a message through. That brings us to the final point — who was the message intended for? My hunch is it was for James Barton.'

The sheriff sat looking at him, saying nothing. At last he reached for the bottle and replenished their glasses.

'Luke,' he said, 'fer weeks I've been goin' round in circles, tryin' to figger this thing out. I'm obliged to yuh. That sure was a piece o' clear thinkin'. Yuh got any more thoughts about it?'

'How long had Pete Connors been in Baronsley?' asked Matson.

'Four, mebbe five years. Why?'

Matson rolled a cigarette and passed the makings to the sheriff before speaking. 'D'yuh know where he'd been before that?'

The lawman shook his head. 'Pete didn't talk much — except about hosses. I never had occasion to question him about anything else.'

'An' supposin' yuh wanted to know about some stranger passin' through your town. Who would yuh see to find out?'

'That's easy,' said the sheriff. 'The

nearest barkeep.'

'Supposin', fer instance, the barkeep hadn't seen him?'

The sheriff scratched his head. 'That ain't likely.' Then he sat upright. 'I see what you're drivin' at. Of course. Most folk comin' into town fer a while would leave their mounts at the livery stable. An' the livery-man would git to know the names o' most of 'em. Next to the barkeep, I reckon I'd go to him fer information.'

'Now, this is a long shot. But, supposin' again that this JB wants to find some *hombre* whose name begins with W — an' that's all we know about him. What does JB do?' Matson looked inquiringly at the sheriff.

'Yuh think he'd git in touch with Connors, two hundred miles away from Makensville?' The lawman's face showed his doubt.

'Mebbe. An' mebbe not jest Connors. We're talkin' about a big cattleman, with a lot o' power, who could pay handsomely fer information. He could well have had several like Pete in places as far apart, say, as Walderswood, Jansen's Ferry, Shotley, Bender's Creek or Bellover. That would cover a hell of a lot o' territory.'

The sheriff got to his feet and reached for his Stetson. 'We'll talk more about this over some grub,' he said. 'I ain't seen Josey in days. Let's mosey across to the restaurant.'

Josey stood by herself at the far end of the dining-room. Her face was grave and worried, but she managed a half-smile as she saw then enter. Within minutes she was serving them.

The lawman gazed up at her. 'What's the matter, Josey?' he asked.

'I'm not sure, Pat,' she said. 'But I don't like a lot of things. There's too many people looking over their shoulders as they walk about. Some of my usual customers are coming in, not talking to me or anyone else, gulping their food down and hurrying out.' She waved a hand at the half-empty room. 'Those that still come in, that is.'

'One thing's fer sure,' said Luke Matson, half jokingly, 'it ain't your cookin' that's keepin' 'em away.' He turned to the sheriff. 'Josey doesn't have any strong competition, does she?'

Stephens shook his head. 'Nope. The hotel serves meals, but Josey can more than match 'em.'

'The hotel's no trouble,' agreed Josey. 'In fact, that Nelson Bush comes in most mornings for his breakfast. But there are a couple of strangers who've taken to hanging about outside some days. Old Billy Welch told me they've been in town about six months now. Jimmy Deken and Sandy Jefferson. Deken can't be more than twenty; he's thin and short; but his hair's nearly grey.' She laughed suddenly. 'He smiles at me when he sees me. He's got a lovely smile.' The laugh faded. 'But Billy reckons he's deadlier than a rattlesnake. Jefferson's old enough to be his father. He's very strong, in a lumbering sort of way, but he seems to be on edge all the time, as though he had something serious to hide.'

She glanced around the room. Matson noticed her clenched hands and how the colour faded from her face.

She seemed to recognize his concern, but the smile she managed hardly reached her lips. When she spoke, it was in a whisper. 'I'm scared, Mr Matson.'

'Where do these two — Deken and Jefferson — hang out?' Stephens's voice seemed trimmed with ice.

Josey put a quick hand on his arm. 'Don't get all het up, Pat. Now you two are back, I'm sure things will improve.'

A customer a few tables away beckoned. She smiled at the sheriff as she turned and left their table.

A minute or two later, she came hurrying back, and Matson saw that she was agitated. 'I forgot,' she said. 'Old Billy sat here 'most all yesterday. He wanted to see you badly. I haven't ever seen him so tense. He seemed to jump every time anyone came in. Anyway, he went out eventually, but he said he'd be in for breakfast today — he reckoned you'd be sure to be here.'

'I was over at the Wilson spread most o' yesterday,' said the sheriff. 'An' I had to catch up with paperwork this mornin'. That's why I missed breakfast.' He smiled apologetically at her.

She shook her head. 'Billy didn't show up this morning. I'd think nothing of it, but he seemed so strange yesterday. Almost frightened. Not like him at all.'

Matson looked at her. There was a pleading look in the woman's brown eyes.

The sheriff took one regretful glance at the mountain of food still on his plate, then he spoke to Luke Matson. 'Let's go.'

Matson sighed and stood up. He saw Josey watching him intently. 'Doesn't need two of us,' he said. 'You stay here, Sheriff. I've had one good meal today. Where do I find the ol' feller?'

The lawman told him, and Josey thanked him with her eyes.

Five minutes later he reached the old man's shack.

All was quiet, but he couldn't open the door. He walked quietly round to the back and looked through a window. Then he saw the reason for the shut door. What looked like a bundle of old clothes lay sprawled across the bottom of it. He waited for a sign of movement, but there was none. He broke the window with the butt of his Colt, smashing the glass until he had space enough to climb into the room.

There would never again be any movement from Billy Welch. The worn, black haft of the knife that stood stiffly upright in the old-timer's back was a deadly witness to that.

11

Matson climbed the steps to the sheriff's office with a heavy heart. It was obvious to him that there was not only a connection between Welch's killing and his joking claim in the Lucky Chance that he knew the identity of the mysterious JB, but that before his death he had been threatened, probably by Pete Connors's killer.

To his surprise, the sheriff was not alone. Huddled in a chair at his side sat Josey Simmonds. She took one look at Matson and buried her face in her hands.

Matson was swift and concise in answer to the sheriff's question. 'Dead, I'm afraid. Knife in the back. Never had a chance.' He looked at the woman. 'Don't take it so hard, Josey. There was nothin' you could've done. He signed his death warrant when he told the sheriff that tall tale in the saloon about knowin' who JB was.'

Josey looked at him wide-eyed. 'But he did know,' she whispered. 'He knew the real 'JB' — and the 'W'. He told me so yesterday. I didn't pay much attention. He was known for his yarns. It was only when he didn't turn up for breakfast that I began to worry. It's too late now.' There were tears in her eyes.

The sheriff's face was white. 'Josey,' he said slowly, 'he didn't tell yuh their names, did he?'

She shook her head. 'No. I asked him, but he wouldn't. Said he was going to tell you or Luke when he saw you.'

Matson turned to the sheriff. The lawman said heavily, 'I know what yuh're thinkin', an' you're right. Billy Welch knew his days were numbered. He wasn't goin' to pass that sentence on to a woman.'

Josey's tears were falling now. 'I should've listened. I didn't realize how serious things were. I would never have thought of anyone killing an old man like him. Not in a million years.'

She clutched at Stephens sitting beside her, an arm still around her shoulder. 'Pat! Oh, Pat! You could be next!'

'Me an' my big mouth,' said the sheriff, obviously annoyed with himself. He put both arms around the now-sobbing Josey, and looked pointedly at Luke Matson.

'There's things that need doin',' said Matson, hurriedly getting to his feet and moving to the door.

But Josey was making a big attempt to compose herself. 'I must get back to the restaurant,' she admitted, standing up. 'Customers still have to be fed, no matter what happens.'

The sheriff stood up with her. 'I ain't lettin' yuh out o' my sight fer the rest o' the day,' he said. 'We'll go together.'

Matson opened the door for them, and then stood aside. They hardly seemed to notice him as they made their way out.

Luke Matson left the office, crossed over to Main Street, and just caught sight of the sheriff and Josey Simmonds as they entered the restaurant. By the time he arrived they had disappeared. He was about to go in when there was a noise from inside. He heard Josey scream.

He eased the Colt from its holster, opened the door noiselessly and slid into the room.

He was in time to see the big man Josey had described as Sandy Jefferson crash to the floor as the sheriff got in a pile-driving right hook. A slightly built man stood by Josey's side, holding her back with one hand while the other casually drew the six-gun from the tied-down holster at his right hip. The lawman had his back to him.

'Yuh wanna turn round slowly, Sheriff? Or would yuh rather die wonderin'?'

'Put your hawgleg down, Deken,' said

Matson from behind the gunman. 'An' git your hands high where I can see 'em.'

Deken stiffened but stayed still. Then his other hand slowly released Josey as she stood motionless.

'Don't move, *hombre*,' said Matson icily. 'Josey, walk away from him — slowly.'

The restaurant owner did as she was told, looking unbelievingly at Deken as she moved.

'I'll tell yuh one more time, Deken,' said Matson. 'Put the six-gun down or I'll gut-shoot yuh, fer thinkin' o' hidin' behind a woman.'

This time the gunman placed his six-gun slowly on the ground, turning round as he straightened up. His lip curled as he saw Matson, but when he spoke it was to the white-faced Josey. He smiled at her.

'Don't yuh worry, ma'am. I ain't figgerin' on killin' either of 'em.' He paused, and the smile widened. 'Yet.'

The sheriff had disarmed his bulky

opponent, and now he picked up Deken's six-gun and stuck it in his belt. He dragged Jefferson to his feet. 'Stand still,' he ordered. 'Don't make any sort o' move. My temper's kind o' jumpy at the moment.'

'What happened?' asked Matson.

'Josey an' me walked through the door,' said the sheriff, 'an' these two *hombres* were sat there each side of it, an' caught me cold as we came in. But the big feller was jest a little over-eager. He spun me round, an' I sorta hit him as I turned.'

Matson looked at Jefferson's swollen jaw and grinned at the lawman. 'Lucky fer him yuh couldn't hit him properly,' he said.

Jefferson snarled at him. 'He was lucky, mister. I'll remember the two o' yuh.'

'Shut up, Sandy,' said Deken. He looked long and hard at the sheriff. 'What're yuh aimin' to do?' He grinned. 'Ain't no dead or wounded — except Sandy here.' He turned to

129

face Matson, the grin still wide. 'Yuh got me off guard, *amigo*. Lucky fer you, I ain't one to bear grudges. Not while there's a lady present, anyway.'

Josey was still standing next to the sheriff. She trembled as Deken looked at her, his smile now fixed.

But Stephens's features had turned to stone. He stepped in front of Josey and clamped a hand on Deken's shoulder, jerking him round so they stood face to face.

'Try that look on me,' he suggested, drawing back his free hand. 'An' I promise you you'll never smile again! Git out, an' take your sidekick with yuh!'

Matson watched the suddenly livid Deken fighting for self-control. At last the gunman managed to speak. 'Jest gimme my Colt, lawman!'

To Matson's horror the sheriff's hand stretched down to the forty-five he had put in his belt. He started to pull it out and made to offer it to Deken.

Matson swore, and his Colt swept

upwards to centre on the gunman.

But Josey Simmonds, eyes wide open in terror, screamed, and screamed again. 'Don't Pat! Don't give him the gun! He'll kill you!'

Stephens froze in his tracks, his fingers now white with tension, the gun in his hand aimed at Deken's heart.

In the sudden silence Matson said, 'Don't make a move, Deken. It could be your last.' His words were easy, almost casual.

But they had an instant effect on the sheriff. In turn, he looked at Deken, and then at Matson, standing quietly there, Colt still drawn, and finally at Josey, eyes huge in her tense face. He pushed the gun back into his belt, moved towards her, and took her hands in his.

Matson looked at them for a moment. Then he waved his Colt in the direction of the door. His tone was frosty. 'You heard what he said, Deken. Git out, an' take Jefferson with yuh.'

The news of Billy Welch's killing had left Baronsley stunned. The customers in the Lucky Chance the next morning crowded round Luke Matson when he came in. Bud Jenning seemed to speak for all of them. 'What happened? Who killed him — an' why?'

'The ol' feller never had a chance,' said Matson. 'Looks like he went to the door, opened it, was knifed in the back, and died at once.'

He looked at the barkeep, behind his bar, shaking his head. 'As to why,' Matson said, 'I reckon that tall tale he told the sheriff was the reason fer the killin'. Someone must have thought the yarn was jest a cover-up, an' that Billy did know who Pete Connors was tryin' to git a message to.'

There was a commotion in the crowd. The burly figure of Rick Pallas pushed his way through to the front. 'Yuh ain't been in Baronsley long, Matson,' he growled. 'But whenever there's a shootin' or a corpse, yuh seem to be around.' He turned to the onlookers behind him. 'This *hombre* was there when Felix Wilson was gunned down. He was there when Pete Connors was killed. An' guess who found ol' Billy Welch's body.'

Matson said, 'Now let's hear the rest of it.'

'What d'yuh mean?'

'How I wasn't totin' a gun when Felix was bushwhacked, but was wearin' one a few hours later. Now yuh listen to me, Pallas. I spent several hours with Wilson, waitin' fer the doctor. I was with the sheriff when Connors was killed; an' it was the sheriff who sent me to investigate when some of his friends were worried about Billy Welch.'

Pallas bellowed in disbelief. 'People here ain't fools. They ain't goin' to believe a no-good killer like you — even if our useless John Law's backin' yuh.'

Matson sighed and pushed himself away from the bar to face Pallas. At the look on his face men backed away from the vicinity.

'Pallas,' Matson said, frosty-eyed, 'yuh reckon you're one tough *hombre* an' this town's eatin' out of your hand. Yuh're jest a broken-down, lyin', bag o' wind. Now, what d'yuh reckon on doin' about that?'

The space between the two and the onlookers widened still further.

Pallas's face purpled. He tried to speak, failed, and his right hand plunged down.

But as his Colt slid from its holster, Matson's was already free and erupting into action. The heavy forty-five slug tore Pallas's weapon from his grasp and smashed it onto the bar-room floor.

There was an unbelieving gasp from the crowd.

Pallas stood rigid, mouth slack, holding his right wrist with his other hand, staring at where his Colt lay out of reach. Then he half turned and looked blankly at Matson.

Matson holstered his Colt. His face

was bleak. 'I could've killed yuh, Pallas.' He looked at the shaken man. 'I should have. If yuh cross me again, I will.'

Rick Pallas turned unsteadily and pushed his way out through the silent spectators. The batwing doors swung noiselessly to behind him.

The tenseness faded from Matson's face as the barkeep pushed a bottle and glass over to him. He nodded his thanks.

Bud Jenning sucked in his breath. 'I still don't believe it,' he said to the men who had clustered around the bar as Pallas slunk from the saloon. 'I still don't believe what I saw. Luke here lets Pallas git his hawgleg halfway out, an' then shoots it out of his fist.' He shook his head and turned to where Matson stood, glass in hand. 'Yuh took a chance, Luke. Pallas ain't no slouch with a gun, an' no one could've blamed yuh if yuh'd killed him. He drew first, an' there ain't no one here can deny that.'

Matson drained his glass. He said

slowly, 'I ain't that fond o' killin', an' I sorta hustled him into drawin'. Leave it at that, Bud. Here,' he pushed the bottle across to the barkeep with a smile, 'yuh look as if one, jest this once, might do yuh a power o' good.'

There was a burst of good-natured laughter from the spectators as Bud Jenning mopped his brow and accepted the invitation. He lifted his glass in salute, but his face was sombre. 'I still reckon that Pallas ain't worth the chance yuh took in lettin' him live. I sure hope yuh don't come to regret it.'

A familiar voice from behind Matson said, 'Bud's right, Luke. Pallas drew first. You've got to watch yore-self from now on.'

Matson swung round and grinned. 'Howdy, Sheriff. Bud, push a clean glass, if you've got such a thing, in Pat's direction. He's plumb swollen up with one o' Josey's breakfasts.'

The sheriff scowled at him, waited, and then tipped a generous measure into his glass and one into the barkeep's. He waved the bottle under Matson's nose. 'You accusin' me o' bein' fat? I got a mind to confiscate this here bottle. Still,' he half-filled Matson's glass, 'I can't take the risk o' bein' shot on a full stomach.'

'Yuh shouldn't have done that,' said the barkeep. 'I warned Luke, here, about the evils o' drink once, an' now he has the gall to suggest my glasses ain't clean. Still, if yuh hadn't filled his glass again I suppose he might have shot both of us.'

He turned away to serve a dozen customers who seemed suddenly to swamp his bar. The sheriff smiled sheepishly at Matson. There was a cheerful, even happy, look on the lawman's rugged face.

A sudden thought crept into Matson's mind. He remembered how much Josey had disliked the times in the sheriff's life when he had been forced into gunplay. But during the incident at the restaurant she had seemed to realize how close to death Patrick Stephens could have been when he almost returned Deken's Colt to him — and she had been the first to scream a warning to the sheriff.

Matson asked quietly, never taking his eyes off the sheriff, 'You had breakfast at Josey's this mornin'?'

The lawman nodded.

'How is she?'

'She's fine,' said the sheriff. 'Fine, but still a little nervous — which is natural, I reckon. In fact, she didn't want me to leave. That's why I'm late. I stayed with her until — until . . . ' He stopped, confusion in his features.

Matson grinned delightedly at him. 'Until she agreed to fix a date,' he suggested. He lifted his glass high. 'I'm mighty glad fer both o' yuh. When will it be?'

'When all this trouble's over,' said the sheriff. 'An' I'm cussed if I can see an end to it yet. Not only that. Baronsley's gittin' bigger each year, an' that means more work fer me.' He looked hard at Matson. 'I've been makin' inquiries.

Seems there's *dinero* available if I need a deputy. What d'yuh say? I'd be glad of your help, an' you'd sure earn your keep.'

Matson thought it over. A few weeks ago, Baronsley would have been a town for riding through, and on to the next, and then the next, and so on. But now, the thought of leaving was unthinkable. Here he would put down roots at last. That had been decided the night at the Bar W when Susan Tate had first kissed him and changed his life for ever.

He looked up at the lawman's earnest, hopeful face and held out his hand. 'You've got yourself a deputy, Pat,' he said.

Stephens smiled in evident satisfaction. 'Let's go on down to the office,' he said. 'I've got a little paperwork to do.'

It was high noon as they walked the short distance from the Lucky Chance to the sheriff's office. The street was deserted and the sun's heat drenched the sidewalk beneath their feet.

'Sure is hot,' said the sheriff,

mopping his face, as they neared the hotel.

'As your deputy,' said Matson, 'I reckon I'd have to claim extra fer workin' this time of the day.'

'You're goin' to be lucky enough to have the benefit o' my years of experience an' wisdom,' said the sheriff, severely. 'You should be payin' me fer the privilege — or at least buyin' the drinks, out o' gratitude.'

Matson pointedly ignored him. They had reached the hotel entrance. A single horse stood at the hitching rail outside. 'That's a nice animal,' said Matson. 'Hell, a poor overworked deputy'd never afford one like that.'

'Nor would a poor overworked sheriff,' quipped Stephens, stopping to have a closer look.

At that moment there came a shout from inside the hotel. 'Johnson! I'll be away mebbe three, four days — mebbe longer!' Nelson Bush dashed from the hotel, vaulted on to the waiting horse, raised an arm in greeting as he caught sight of the two men, and disappeared in a cloud of dust.

But Matson had seen Bush's face — a strange mixture of horror, fear, and anger — as the hotel owner leapt into the saddle. And once again a feeling of uncertainty about the man crept into his mind. He walked out into the middle of the dusty street, and did not move until Nelson Bush was out of sight.

12

By the time Luke Matson had seen Nelson Bush ride out of sight, the sheriff had joined his new deputy. 'Mind tellin' me what's on your mind, Luke?' he asked.

'Ain't nothin' I can rightly put words to,' admitted Matson. 'Jest somethin' in the way Bush looked — an' especially in the way he left his hotel in a hell of a rush, as if the Devil himself was behind him.'

The sheriff looked thoughtful. 'He was yellin' a message to that clerk of his — Johnson,' he said. 'I don't think the clerk saw us. Let's go in an' have a word with the feller.'

The clerk looked up when they reached the hotel reception desk.

Matson said, 'Mornin' to yuh, is your boss in?'

The clerk shook his head. 'No. An' I

don't expect him back fer three or four days — mebbe longer.'

Matson said, 'That long? Did he say where he's goin'?'

'I ain't sure,' said the clerk. 'He's been talkin' o' buyin' another hotel, Bellover way. But he was in too much of a hurry to say anything, except how long he'd be away. Bust in through the back door, yelled a few words at me, an' the next thing I heard was his hoss goin' hell fer leather.'

'It ain't no matter,' said the sheriff. 'I'll see him when he comes back. An' if he's goin' as far as Bellover he may well be away longer than he said.' He looked at the clerk. 'Reckon you'll be on your own. Well, if yuh run into any trouble, let me or Mr Matson, here, know.'

'I'm obliged, Sheriff.' The clerk left his seat and came to the hotel main door with them. 'If I hear when Mr Bush is comin' back, I'll let yuh know.'

They were on the way back to the office when a horseman came round the corner at a gallop. When he saw the sheriff he reined in in a cloud of dust.

'Sheriff,' he yelled, 'you're wanted out at the Wilson spread. John Wilson's dead. Knifed in his bed.' He didn't wait for an answer but swung his mount round and headed back the way he'd come.

The lawman looked at Matson. 'Come into the office,' he said. 'This won't take a minute, an' it'll make everything legal.'

Once inside he pulled open a drawer and rummaged through the contents. Finally, he grunted and tossed a star across to Matson. 'Put that on,' he said. 'Right. Now lift up your right arm. Swear. That's it. You'd already accepted the job, so there ain't no more formalities. You're my deputy.'

His face hardened. 'Whoever knifed John must've come from Baronsley,' he said. 'I'll stay here an' see what I can find out. I'd like yuh to ride out to the Bar W an' see what happened.' He shook his head. 'God knows what Martha Wilson's goin' through.'

Luke Matson dismounted at the Bar W ranch-house. As he did so the door opened and Susan Tate appeared. He walked up the porch steps to her. She clung to him for a brief moment. Her eyes were sombre. 'I'm glad you're here, Luke. So glad. Martha and Janet are almost out of their minds. Three men fired on us from the front of the house. My father's men fought them off, but — but when they'd gone we found that someone had got in through the back and murdered John. He was still alive when the doctor came but he died minutes later.'

In the living-room Doc Parkinson sat at the table, shirt sleeves rolled up, face ashen. When Matson and Susan appeared he saw the star on Luke's vest. 'You're here in your official capacity, Mr Matson? How long have you been a deputy?'

'A matter of hours,' said Matson, drily. 'The sheriff is investigatin' another killin'. Old Billy Welch was found dead yesterday mornin' in his cabin — a knife in his back.'

'Billy Welch?' said the doctor, incredulously. 'Who would want to kill a harmless old-timer like him?'

'Who would want to kill Pete Connors? Or John Wilson? Or damn near kill Felix Wilson, fer that matter?' As he spoke, Matson sat down at the table with the doctor and Susan.

Susan said, quietly, 'How are Janet and Martha now, Doctor?'

He shook his head. 'I've given them both something to help them sleep. They should be all right till morning. But I can't even guess at how they're going to make out. Felix is the only living relative they have left — and if anything should happen to him it could finish both of them.'

'Felix is taking it badly,' said Susan. 'He's insisted on taking a turn at guarding the house, even though he's only half fit.'

'Felix was already on the mend,' said

the doctor. 'He's probably better off on his feet than lying in bed feeling helpless. As long as he doesn't go off at half cock.' He pushed his chair back and picked up his bag. He shook his head. 'It's a bad business. I'll go into Baronsley and make all the arrangements. There's nothing more I can do here at the moment. I'll be in tomorrow, Susan.' As he reached the door he stopped and swung round to face Matson.

'Mr Matson,' he said. 'Have you still got a copy of the message that Pete Connors left?'

Matson looked at him. 'I have,' he said. 'Why?'

'Show it to Felix. He might be able to help you. Just a thought.' He closed the door and was gone.

★   ★   ★

After the evening meal Susan made her way upstairs to see Janet and her mother. Andrew Tate's men had given

Matson the details of the previous night's attack, confirming Susan's account. The short, sharp fight had taken them by surprise, and John Wilson's killing had been swift and silent. There were no excuses. The attackers had been clever and ruthless and had outwitted the defenders.

Now, as Susan and Matson sat together again by the fire in the living-room they were joined by Felix Wilson. Even in the lamplight, he looked pale and drawn, but there was no weakness in his voice, nor in his intention to help guard the house, judging by the Colt in the well-worn holster tied down at his right thigh.

He was a little taken aback at the sight of Matson and the star he wore, but his tone was friendly. 'I owe yuh, friend. I ain't ever goin' to fergit yuh bluffin' that feller with the Winchester. But fer you I'd have been shakin' hands with St Peter fer sure.' He sat silent for a while, then he said quietly, his voice flat, 'I reckon someone was after me again last night — an' got the wrong man. An' wrecked the lives o' two innocent women. The dirty sidewinder crawled in an' killed a man who couldn't move hand or foot, a man who raised me as his own an' stood by me through thick an' thin.' He stopped speaking and sat facing the two of them, his face in his hands.

Matson waited until Wilson looked up again. Then he said, 'D'yuh have any idea who's after yuh — or why?'

Wilson shook his head. 'Nope. John an' I spent most of our time like most small ranchers — workin'. Ain't had no cause to upset folks; not knowingly anyway.'

Susan said, 'What about Pallas, Felix?'

'Far as I know, he ain't got no reason. I was shot with a Winchester. So was John, and then he was knifed. I ain't ever seen Pallas with one or the other. Fists or six-guns — that's his limit. I can take him with either, an' he knows it.'

There was nothing boastful in the statement. Just the words of a man who was sure of himself and his capabilities. Matson was impressed. He said, 'Doc Parkinson suggested I show yuh this.' He put the copy of Connors's message on the table.

Wilson studied the note intently. He said, 'Where'd yuh git this?'

'You were unconscious at the time an' won't have heard,' said Matson. 'But Pete Connors was shot down a few days ago. Before he died he scrawled a message in his own blood on his stable wall. This is it.'

' "Tell JB where W — ",' Wilson read the words out, a frown on his face. He paused, and then understanding crept into his features. He looked questioningly at Susan.

'Yes,' she said. 'Martha told me the whole story. And then she asked me to tell Luke, because she was at her wits' end and thought only he and the sheriff could help her.'

'My father's name was — is — James

Barton,' said Wilson, slowly, pausing after each word as though he found it distasteful. 'Is he the 'JB' in this note?'

Matson put the note back in his pocket. 'It's jest a hunch,' he admitted.

'Yuh reckon he had a hand in these killings — an' tried to kill me?'

Matson shook his head. 'No. I ain't got any evidence o' that. Let's say he's jest a link. An' the only one at the moment. You're the first one to be bushwhacked — 'JB' is your father, though he doesn't recognize yuh as his son, an' yuh can't even remember what he looks like. Pete Connors is shot down — an' he tries to leave a message fer 'JB'. Pore ol' Billy Welch is the next to go — and he shouted his mouth off in the Lucky Chance that he knew who 'JB' was. Even though he admitted at the time that it was a tall tale to catch the sheriff, someone could have believed he really did know.'

'It ain't much of a peg to hang a hat on,' said Wilson. 'On the other hand, I can't recall many folk with those initials. Have yuh got any ideas about who carried out the actual killings?'

'No. Nor why. An' I reckon that's the important question,' said Matson. 'Why were they all killed? If we can find an answer to that, mebbe we'll be on the right path, instead o' workin' blind.'

Felix Wilson hesitated for a while. Then he said, 'I'm sorry to hear about Pete Connors. An' after what you've told me, this might interest yuh. A couple o' days before I was bushwhacked I was talkin' to Pete outside his livery stable. Now, Pete wasn't normally what you'd call a talkative sort of feller. An', now I come to think of it, he didn't seem quite his usual self, a touch nervy even. He was tellin' me about his years workin' fer a big ranch south o' here, an' how when he left them to come to Baronsley he stayed on the payroll, passin' on information about a list o' people the owner was interested in if they happened to pass through Baronsley at any time — they were mostly other owners, strangers to

Pete, so he jest did what he was paid fer and asked no questions. He reckoned the man had someone like him in most all the towns in the area from Shotley down to Walderswood and Makensville.'

He stood up and walked over to the window, and stayed motionless for a while. Then he turned and came back to his chair. He looked hard at Matson and Susan. He said, 'Before Pete Connors went back into the livery stable, there seemed to be somethin' on his mind. When I asked him, he hesitated, but anyway, at last he told me what it was. A letter had come from his previous boss askin' Pete fer information about me an' the Bar W.'

Matson said, 'Yuh weren't a stranger, an' Pete didn't fancy spyin' on yuh.'

'That's right. He told me that the man jest wanted to know how I was doin'; how I was leadin' my life; whether I was a good rancher an' trustworthy — that sort o' thing. It was something of a shock to me — though Pete wouldn't have known why — but I

153

managed to laugh, an' said if that was all, he could go ahead an' send in his report. That seemed to take a load off his mind, an' he thanked me an' went back in.'

Matson and Susan exchanged glances. It was Susan who asked the question. 'Felix, what was the owner's name?'

Felix Wilson shrugged his shoulders. 'It was James Barton.'

13

Luke Matson had a further question for Felix Wilson. He looked across the table to where the young man sat, quiet and pale now, and said, 'Pete Connors had no idea yuh were Barton's son?'

Wilson nodded. 'I'd bet money on it. Likewise, I ain't got any reason to think well of my father, but I don't think he's behind the *hombre* who tried to kill me. If he had been, he wouldn't have bothered to git information about me — that don't make any kind o' sense.'

'An' Pallas? You've already said yuh don't suspect him.'

'The feller who plugged me was an expert with a Winchester — in the dark, too. I wouldn't rate Pallas in bad light. I reckon he's jest a close-up six-gun man.'

'How about Ingham?'

'Nope.' Wilson's tone was definite.

'The bushwhacker was crouchin', but Ingham would look as big crouchin' as standin' upright. An' the bushwhacker was nowhere near that size.'

'I've seen Pallas an' Ingham together,' said Matson. 'An' Ingham, an' Nelson Bush. What d'yuh know about him?'

Felix Wilson shifted in his chair. 'Only thing I know about him,' he said, 'is he looks more at home on a horse than he does trampin' about hotel corridors.'

'The sheriff an' me had a run-in with a couple of other fellers,' said Matson. 'Deken an' Jefferson.'

'They're linked up with Ingham, somewhere. Don't seem to work but always have plenty *dinero*. An' Deken's all poison, through an' through. But if he'd been the bushwhacker, I don't reckon you'd have bluffed him. Anyway, if he'd thought I was dead he'd have shot me again jest fer the hell of it.'

'We need a reason,' said Matson. 'Why would someone spend so much time an' effort in tryin' to git rid o' yuh? Yuh got any ideas?'

Wilson laughed. 'I ain't ever been what yuh might call a hell-raiser,' he said. 'About the only man I can't stomach is Pallas — an' he can't stand me. But he ain't goin' to do anything about it, an', unless he calls me, neither am I. John brought me up in what he considered the right way. An' when he thought I was ready he taught me to use a Colt an' a Winchester an' my fists, an' to know I was in the right before I used any of 'em.'

Susan said, 'Luke, it's getting late. Felix's been on his feet long enough for one day. But you'll stay here tonight, won't you?'

Matson got up from his chair. 'I'd like to, Susan, but I sorta promised Pat I'd git back. He's worried sick about these killings.'

He said good-night to Felix. At the door, Susan kissed him and then held him close. She was trembling. 'Luke, be careful. I couldn't bear to lose you now.'

He put his arms around her. 'Hush now. We'll find a way out of this before long, I promise yuh. An' that day can't come soon enough.'

* ★ ★

Baronsley was in almost complete darkness when he returned. Here and there lamps glimmered in a losing fight with the shadows, but there was no sign of life, no movement in the hushed street. But a light still showed in the sheriff's office, as he dismounted at the foot of the steps. He pushed open the door and went in. Stephens looked up as he entered. In the lamplight the sheriff's face seemed pale and drawn, but he smiled at Matson and pushed a bottle and glass towards him. 'Glad to see yuh back, Luke. Did yuh find out anything?'

Matson shook his head. 'Not much. Felix Wilson is out o' bed and carryin' a six-gun again. He still says he ain't got any ideas about who's behind the killings — an' I believe him. He's a straight-talkin' young feller.'

He drained his glass and put it down, shaking his head when the sheriff motioned towards the bottle. 'There's two things I'm sure about: Felix Wilson doesn't know why he's bein' hunted — he reckons John Wilson was killed by mistake fer him. An' James Barton ain't responsible fer the killings either — but I'm sure he's the key to them. Felix met Connors a day or so before the liveryman's death, and found he had been employed by James Barton. Barton had written for some information about Felix, but Connors wasn't happy about goin' behind Felix's back. Felix laughed and told him to go ahead.'

Matson paused. 'But, there's someone else, even if he is a real long shot.'

Sheriff Stephens looked interested. 'Who?'

'Somethin' Susan said over at the Bar W put me on the track. As yuh know, Barton has another son — Felix

Wilson's half-brother. He ran away from home when he was fifteen, a couple of years before Felix was born. That's all she knows about him. According to Martha Wilson, her sister Helen never even mentioned his name.'

'That's sure enough a hell of a long shot,' said the sheriff. 'Why would he want to kill a half-brother — always supposin' he does — who was thrown out o' the family when he was only a few months old?'

'Look at it this way,' said Matson. 'When all this trouble started, Felix was the hard-workin' adopted son of a small rancher, an' well liked in the neighbourhood. An' that was all. No reason fer anyone to go to a lot o' trouble an' expense to kill him. But Barton must be gittin' an old man. A rich old man. He has two sons — one he don't recognize as his; an' one who disappeared years ago. He's been makin' inquiries about Felix. Supposin' that first of all, some time ago, he managed to trace the other one.'

'I'm with you,' said the sheriff. 'He's a rancher, in a big way. Blood's thicker than water. He's made his mind up. He's goin' to leave the lot to one son or both.'

'An' supposin',' said Matson, 'he told the older one that he wasn't goin' to make up his mind until he had made inquiries about his half-brother?'

'Then,' said the sheriff, looking at his deputy with something close to admiration, 'I got to hand it to yuh, Luke. To some, money could be a powerful reason fer anything — even murder.'

'As I said, it's only a long shot,' said Matson. 'D'yuh reckon it's worth following up?'

'It's our only chance as far as I can see,' said Stephens, getting up, and stifling a yawn as he did so. 'Let's git some sleep. I reckon yuh must be as tired as I am. Tomorrow I'll hold the fort here. See what else yuh can dig up.' He yawned openly as he crossed the room and rolled into his bunk.

Luke Matson sat at the table, his head in his hands, feeling the tiredness creeping over him. But time and time again he went over in his mind the few far-fetched theories, and even fewer facts, that represented the only attempts at the identities of those responsible for three deaths and a near miss.

By the time the sheriff was snoring opposite him, Matson gave up the struggle, and stretched out in his own bunk, waiting for sleep to overtake him. His last conscious thought was that surely a break must come sooner rather than later. Sooner rather than . . .

14

Josey's Restaurant was packed as usual the next morning when Luke Matson went in for breakfast. He was waiting for the sheriff to join him, and Josey had already taken the order for their meal, when a stranger came in. Luke studied him as he stood in the doorway, a lean, wide-shouldered man in his forties, hollow-cheeked, coal-black hair and moustache, a couple of inches over six foot tall and well dressed. But what caught Matson's eye particularly were the sneer on the stranger's face as he glanced around the room, and the butts of twin Colts, half hidden by his coat.

His gaze appeared to fasten on a small table against the wall at the opposite side of the room, situated where anyone entering the restaurant could be seen easily, thought Matson. The stranger seemed to nod in satisfaction and strode across the room.

He halted at the table and glared at the old man sitting there, happily concentrating on his half-eaten breakfast. It was obvious that the old fellow hadn't seen him.

The next moment, Matson stiffened in his chair.

'Hey you!' The stranger reached down and shook the old man by the shoulder. 'I wanna sit here.'

There was an empty chair opposite the old man. He half choked, and then pointed to it, spluttering, 'Help yourself, friend.'

At that moment, Josey came out of her kitchen with a plateful of breakfast in either hand. She stopped in her tracks.

'What's going on, then?'

The stranger ignored her. He grasped the old man by the shoulder and pulled him to his feet. 'Yuh don't hear good, ol'-timer. I want *your* chair.'

Josey stepped in between them.

As she did so, Matson left his seat.

The restaurant owner was shaking with anger. She screamed at the stranger, 'Leave the old fellow alone! Get out!'

The man's face darkened. He snarled, 'Keep out o' this, woman,' and swung round, sweeping her aside.

Josey staggered, the plates crashing from her hands. But Matson was at her side. He caught her and kept her on her feet. He looked round.

The old man had taken the opportunity to sit down again. Matson guided Josey into the vacant chair opposite him, then turned and faced the stranger.

The babble of noise in the room suddenly hushed.

The deputy's voice was mild. 'Yuh don't hear good either, mister.' The mildness vanished. There was now a threat in the flat tones. 'The lady told yuh to git out. Now I'm tellin' yuh.'

The stranger tensed. 'You're gittin' out of your depth, feller. No star-totin', interferin' deputy tells me what I can do.'

Luke Matson sighed and his right shoulder twitched. Some of those nearest him swore afterwards that he hadn't moved, but there was a Colt in his hand and the stranger's swoop down to his own holster had stopped halfway.

Matson said bleakly, 'Have it your way. I ain't tellin' yuh what to do. But if that gunbelt don't hit the floor pronto, yuh ain't ever goin' to walk again.'

For a moment the stranger stood stiff and silent. Then he stooped slowly, his hands going to his waist, and belt and forty-fives slid to the ground. All the time, his eyes never left Matson's face.

And, sitting at the table, Josey shivered.

'Yuh're a fool, Deputy,' the stranger said. 'Yuh should've killed me when yuh had the chance.'

Matson holstered his Colt and picked up the gunbelt. 'I don't like killin',' he said. 'But I could make an exception in your case.' He turned to the woman. 'What d'yuh want me to do with this *hombre*, Josey?'

She looked at the stranger and shuddered, her face white. 'Just get him out of here, Luke. Please.'

He smiled at her. 'I'll take him down to the office, Josey. Somethin' must've come up fer Pat to miss his breakfast, but I reckon he'll be there, an' he can decide what to do.'

He looked at the stranger. 'That reminds me. Yuh ruined two of Josey's breakfasts. The sheriff might jest decide to have yuh strung up fer that.'

There was a chorus of agreement from the customers sitting rigid at their tables, eyes fixed on their new deputy.

Matson waved a hand in their general direction. 'Don't let your food git cold,' he said. 'This *hombre* ain't worth it.'

On the way to the sheriff's office, the stranger spoke only once. 'There ain't nothin' your sheriff can hold me on. An' you an' me have got some unfinished business.'

'Yuh may have to wait a while,' said Luke Matson. 'Our sheriff ain't a forgivin' sort o' man, an' he ain't goin' to take kindly to you upsettin' Josey. Yuh see, they're plannin' on gittin' married.'

The door to the office was half open. Matson pushed the stranger ahead of him up the steps and inside. To his surprise three men sat in the room with Sheriff Stephens. Two had the appearance of hardened gunslingers. The third was a bent figure of a once-big man, probably in his late seventies, hunched in his chair, only his eyes appearing to have movement and life.

At the sight of Matson and his companion one of the gunslingers came to his feet, hand moving stealthily towards the holster tied down low on his right thigh.

There was a growled command from the old man. 'Sit down yuh fool!'

At first it seemed that his order would be disobeyed. But, with a grudging look on his face, the gunslinger half turned towards the stranger, and Matson saw the barely perceptible nod the latter gave him.

At once, the gunslinger sank back into his chair.

The old man turned his attention to Matson. 'Why did yuh bring him here?' he rasped.

Matson ignored him. He pushed the stranger through into a cell and locked the door, paying no attention to his curses. Then he went back into the office and dropped the man's gunbelt into a desk drawer.

The three men at the table watched him unblinkingly.

They must have completely forgotten the presence of the sheriff, he thought, because, as he turned round, Pat Stephens got to his feet, moved over to a rack, pulled down a shotgun and loaded it. He kept standing, the shotgun cradled comfortably in his arms.

'Ain't nothin' like a scatter-gun to help keep a discussion goin' on in a peaceable manner,' he observed amiably.

There were sour looks on three faces. But the old man looked up at the deputy. 'I asked yuh a question,' he said.

'Who is he? An' what's he to you?' Matson noted that the old man's tone was considerably quieter now.

'His name's Lance Murkin, an' he's my *segundo*, an' I want him out,' was the answer. 'What's the charge?'

'Charges. I ain't figgered 'em all out yet,' said Matson. With an eye on the sheriff, he gave an account of the incidents in Josey's Restaurant. As he finished, he saw the rising anger in Stephens's face.

But the old man had grown impatient. 'You two,' he said to his companions, 'git the hell out of it. Come back in an hour.'

He waited until they had gone, then he turned to the sheriff. 'Yuh won't need that shotgun,' he said. 'Heaven knows, I ain't a danger to anyone any more. I'll pay any fines. But I need Murkin. Jest let me git him out o' here.' He stopped short, gasping for breath. Then he said, almost apologetically, one hand to his chest, 'I've got a wrong to put right an' precious little time to do it.'

'Why d'yuh need him?' Matson asked.

The answer was frank. 'Fer protection mostly. At my age yuh can't depend on your own physical strength. Yuh have to pay fer it. A man who makes a lot o' money makes a lot of enemies. An' I got to keep alive fer a while yet.'

'An' Murkin ain't here to go lookin' fer trouble on your behalf?'

'Nope.'

Matson thought for a while. Then he looked at the sheriff. Stephens nodded. Matson said, 'I'll do a deal with yuh. Yuh can have Murkin. But if he puts a foot wrong in Baronsley I'll have him back in here without warnin'. An' yuh'll be with him. The same goes fer his two *compadres*. There's been more than enough killings here already.'

The old man nodded. 'I'll keep a tight rein on all of 'em. Though sometimes I git the idea that even that's gittin' harder as I git older.'

Matson took a bunch of keys and went back to the cell.

Lance Murkin scowled at him from where he sat on the edge of a bunk.

The deputy opened the door. 'I'm releasin' yuh on the word o' your boss,' he said. 'Any trouble an' you'll share a cell with him. That's the deal. Savvy?'

Back in the office he handed Murkin his guns and gunbelt, and watched as he buckled them on. Then he said, his voice expressionless, 'When you've finished here, Murkin, if yuh still feel yuh want to call me, I'll be happy to oblige yuh.'

Murkin froze and his face darkened.

The old man said, and now there was ice in his voice, 'Draw a gun on a lawman while you're in this town, an' you're through. An' that goes fer your two sidekicks. Yuh go an' fetch them out of whatever saloon they're in, an' the three o' yuh wait fer me in the hotel.'

For a moment the two locked eyes,

and then, with a scowl at Matson and the sheriff, Murkin turned on his heel.

The sound of his footsteps died away. The sheriff looked steadily at the old man. 'It's no business o' mine to tell a man how to run his affairs,' he said. 'But in your place I'd shore be watchin' my back, day an' night.'

The old man said, 'I take that as friendly advice, an' I thank yuh fer it, Sheriff, but I got to play the cards I'm dealt.' He got up from his seat.

The sheriff lifted a hand. He produced a bottle and glasses. 'Sit down a while, friend,' he said. 'As sheriff, I reckon it part o' my job to lend a hand in this town to anyone needin' it — even strangers passin' through. Law-abidin' ones that is.'

He half-filled the three glasses, and raised his own to Matson and the old man.

'Now,' he said, 'I ain't aimin' to pry, but supposin' yuh tell us your name an' what you're doin' here in Baronsley?'

The old man hesitated.

In the silence, Matson put his glass down on the table. There was a smile on his face. 'I thought yuh would've guessed, Pat,' he said.

'Meet Mr Barton. Mr James Barton.'

15

James Barton was shocked to hear of the killing of Pete Connors. Connors had indeed sent in his report on Felix Wilson, and that was why Barton had made the long trip to Baronsley. He had discovered some time before that Felix's mother had not been unfaithful, and remorse had forced him into action.

'I ain't makin' excuses about the way I treated his mother,' he said. 'It's too late fer that. But I got to make it up in some way to Helen's boy. I ain't seen my other son since he was fifteen, but I got in touch with him through a lawyer feller a year or two back an' told him he'd git the ranch when I died. Then I found out about Felix. I let the lawyer know that I would now be leavin' the ranch between the two. There would be plenty fer both of 'em. Accordin' to the lawyer the older boy was happy with this, though he still wouldn't see me.'

'You had no idea before yuh came here,' said the sheriff, 'that three men had died and the only link between them was your name?'

'No idea at all,' said Barton. 'I've never been in Baronsley before. How d'yuh work out that my name was the only link?'

Matson said, 'Felix Wilson was bushwhacked but survived. John Wilson was murdered, an' Felix reckons that he himself was the real target, though he didn't know why. Pete Connors was killed because he knew who yuh were. Billy Welch was killed because he boasted that he knew who yuh were. An' Pete tried desperately to leave a message for yuh.' He pulled from his pocket his copy of Connors's message.

The rancher peered at it. 'My eyes aren't so good now,' he said. He bent down, his face a few inches from the paper. Slowly he spelled out the words: 'Tell JB where W — '.

He straightened up and looked at Matson. 'Where'd yuh git this?'

'When Pete was dyin' he scrawled those words in his own blood on the livery-stable wall. I made a copy.'

'Give Pete Connors a job to do, an' he'd move heaven an' earth to finish it. He'd never met him, but I'd asked him to let me know if he ever saw or heard of my eldest son.' Barton handed the note back to Matson, and sat silent, shaking his head. He spoke softly, almost to himself, and Matson had to strain to hear the words.

'The man is dyin', an' he ain't even thinkin' of himself. He's tryin' to git a message to me — a message to a no-good father about the whereabouts of a no-good son. An' fer that someone kills him.'

He turned to Matson, surprising the deputy. Barton seemed to have suddenly shed the years that had been shackling him.

His voice almost boomed in the confines of the sheriff's office. 'I've only got one way to help yuh. Three murders, yuh say, an' one near killin'. I'll put up a thousand dollars reward fer the capture of whoever's responsible fer each one. There'll be four thousand dollars in your local bank in the mornin'.'

The sheriff said, softly, 'We sure appreciate your help, Mr Barton. Jest one question. Who's the 'W' in Pete Connors's message?'

Luke Matson watched closely as some of the fire died out of the old rancher's eyes, but his voice was steady as he answered, 'Warren. Warren Barton. My eldest son. I ain't seen him in over twenty years.'

* * *

At dawn the next day, Luke Matson saddled up and headed for the Bar W. There he found that Susan Tate was at the Triangle T, but Martha and Janet Wilson, though still grief-stricken over the murder, had recovered sufficiently to listen to the reason for his visit.

They and Felix invited him into the living-room. Matson wasted no time. He said to Felix, 'Your father's in Baronsley. He's at the hotel, an' wants to see yuh — if you're willin'.'

Felix sat still, his face expressionless. After a while he turned and looked at Martha.

She shook her head. 'Before all this trouble, I would have said no. But now — well I think you should at least see him and hear what he has to say. He must be an old man by now, and maybe — maybe . . . ' Her eyes filled with tears.

Janet pressed her mother's hands in hers. 'Hush now,' she said. 'Hush.' She looked at her adopted brother. 'I think you should see him, too, Felix.'

He smiled at them. 'You've made my mind up fer me.' He turned to the deputy. 'All right, Luke. I'll see him. Are yuh ready to ride?'

Matson said, 'Are Andrew Tate's men still here?'

'One in the house; two helpin' outside,' said Felix. 'Why?'

'I reckon it'd be better fer Mr Barton to come here, alone. I'll ride in and bring him back. I don't know why, but I think he'd be safer here than in Baronsley. He brought three of his men with him: his *segundo*, Lance Murkin, an' two buckaroos who wouldn't be seen dead punchin' cows.'

'An' yuh don't reckon to bring them here?'

Matson grinned at him and stood up. 'I've already had a run-in with Murkin. An' put him in jail to cool off. I git the impression that there's somethin' goin' on that your father doesn't know about — an' Murkin's tied up with it. Anyway, I'd better be goin'.'

An hour later Matson left his horse at the livery stable in Baronsley's Main Street. As he reached the door, he heard footsteps approaching, and then a voice he recognized as Matthew Ingham's.

'Hell, *amigo*, let the ol' man think

180

he's still the boss. Jest fer a few days more. Then yuh can deal with the other two.'

The other voice was familiar, laced as it was with hate. 'I'll wait. But when it's over I'm killin' me a lawman.'

Cautiously Matson looked out through the part-open door. Ingham and Lance Murkin were heading towards the hotel, side by side. As he watched, the pair went in through the hotel entrance. He stayed where he was. He didn't want Murkin to see him meeting James Barton.

But almost as the door closed behind them, it opened again suddenly and Murkin and Ingham reappeared, Murkin looking flustered.

Matson followed them at a distance until he saw them entering Ingham's saloon, the Spanish Bull. At that, he turned on his heel and retraced his steps to the hotel.

The clerk looked up as he came in. 'Good mornin', Mr Matson,' he said. 'Mr Barton is waitin' to see yuh.'

'Thanks, I'll go up.' Matson reached the door. A thought struck him. 'By the way, when is that boss o' yours comin' back?'

The clerk seemed to fidget a little at the question. Then he said, 'Well, he was supposed to be returnin' yesterday, but there was a message yesterday afternoon sayin' he would be held up for another four or five days.' He looked at the deputy. 'I shouldn't say so, but if it's important I could probably get a message to him for yuh.'

Matson shook his head. 'Thanks, it's jest a routine matter.' Then he suddenly realized that what had flashed into his mind concerning the hotel keeper was far from routine. Far-fetched — but not routine.

When he entered his room, Barton stood up. 'Sit down, Mr Matson,' he said. 'I'm obliged to yuh fer the trouble you're takin'.'

'No trouble, Mr Barton,' said the deputy, accepting the glass of whiskey the rancher pushed towards him. 'I've jest seen the Wilsons. An' they're willin' to see yuh. They would've come into Baronsley, but I reckon they'd be safer where they are. Not only that, I reckon you'd be safer there too.'

Barton looked surprised. 'You think I'm in danger?'

The deputy nodded. 'It's a possibility. You brought three men with yuh.' He looked hard at the rancher. 'How far d'yuh trust them? In a tight spot, who'd they take orders from — you or Lance Murkin?'

The knuckles on Barton's gnarled hands turned white. But his voice was controlled. 'That's a strange question, Mr Matson.'

Luke Matson sighed. Barton wasn't the first rancher who had reached old age and found his power slipping away — or his past catching up on him. He was silent for a moment, and then he said, 'Back in the office yuh ordered one o' your men to sit down when I came in with Murkin. He obeyed yuh — but not until your *segundo* nodded.'

183

'Took me months to see the signs,' admitted Barton frankly, with an admiring look at the deputy. 'Then yuh come in and read 'em in seconds.' He picked up his glass and drained it. 'Hell, the way I see it, Murkin thinks he's got me treed, an' he's jest waitin' fer me to cash in my chips before he makes his play. I've got two sons. Both of 'em hate my guts. But I'm determined that I'll split the ranch between the two of 'em.' He pulled the bottle towards him and splashed whiskey into Matson's glass and his own.

The deputy lifted his drink. When he put the glass down it was empty. He looked at the rancher. 'Time to go, Mr Barton. By the way d'yuh know a feller called Ingham — Matthew Ingham?'

Barton shook his head. 'No. Why? Should I?'

'Jest a thought.' Matson stood up. 'Or Rick Pallas?' He hesitated a few seconds. 'Or Nelson Bush?'

At the last name, Barton nodded. 'He

owns this hotel. But I haven't ever met him, an' I've never heard of the other two.'

Matson opened the door and waited for Barton to join him. As they made their way across to the livery stable, the deputy said, 'Your *segundo*, Lance Murkin, how long have yuh known him?'

'Three, four years. Why?'

Matson opened the livery-stable door. Once inside, he stopped with the door three-quarter closed and beckoned Barton to his side.

'How far can yuh see down the street?'

The rancher said, 'My eyes ain't what they used to be. But I reckon I can pick out that saloon, four, mebbe five hundred yards away.'

'That's the Spanish Bull,' said the deputy. 'Now, when I came in to see yuh, I left my hoss here. I was comin' out when I heard Ingham's voice.' He went on to tell Barton of Ingham's conversation with the other man —

without mentioning his name — and how the two had gone into the hotel, and had come out again almost immediately. He finished by saying, 'I stood where yuh are now an' watched them go down the street and walk into that saloon.'

'Did yuh know the other man?' Barton's voice was bleak.

Matson looked at the old rancher and saw the lines deepen in his face. 'I did,' he said softly. 'Yes. It was your *segundo*.'

★ ★ ★

When they reached the Bar W, Matson and Barton dismounted. At the porch steps, Barton hesitated. But as he did so, the door opened and Felix and Janet Wilson appeared, with Martha close behind them.

Matson watched as the old rancher faced the three.

Finally Barton turned to where Martha stood, stiff and white-faced, her eyes fixed on him. 'Yuh'll be Helen's sister,' he said. 'Well, I listened to the wrong people an' did her an' our son a great injustice. I'm an old man, an' my faults will die with me. But there may be some way — ' He broke off for a moment, his eyes never leaving her face. He shook his head. 'You're her sister,' he said. 'An' I reckon you suffered most. I'll understand if yuh tell me to go — but I came here in hope, though I don't deserve it.'

Martha looked at him, at Matson, and at Felix and her daughter, and finally back at the rancher again, this time as though she was seeing him through different eyes.

The colour flared in her face. 'I'm forgetting my manners,' she said. 'Keeping people waiting outside, indeed. Come in, Mr Barton, and you, Mr Matson. There's coffee on the stove.'

Once inside the living-room she waited until they all sat down, and then she disappeared into the kitchen. She reappeared a few minutes later with a tray of coffee, and placed it carefully on the table. Then she sat down with them, facing Barton.

Matson watched the varying emotions crossing her features, but her voice was steady when she finally spoke. 'It must have been important to you to come all this way, after all these years, to speak to us, Mr Barton.' It was as much a question as a statement.

'It's the most important thing in my life.' Barton lifted his head as he spoke, then turned and looked directly at Felix. 'All the talkin' in the world ain't goin' to change the past, boy. All I ask is fer yuh to listen to what I'm goin' to say, an' then to make up your own mind. After that, if yuh want me to go — I'll go.'

Felix looked steadily at the speaker, and it struck Matson that there was a likeness in the two of them, a fearlessness in the young man that matched a similar trait in the old rancher, though in Barton's case it was darkened by a lifetime of striving for power.

But when Felix finally spoke there was almost a gentleness in his voice, as though he realized what it had cost this proud old man to admit his private failings in public.

'Go ahead, sir, an' take all the time yuh need. I reckon this ain't a journey yuh undertook lightly.'

He had treated the rancher with respect, thought Matson, and at the same time avoided calling him father. And Barton had seemed as much relieved as surprised at the tone of his voice.

At that moment Matson realized he was present at what was turning out to be a private family party. He got to his feet.

He looked at Martha Wilson. 'If you'll excuse me, Mrs Wilson, I need to have a few words with Mr Tate's men before I go back to town.'

Outside, near the barn, he saw a figure, leaning against a tree, a Winchester cradled comfortably in his

189

arms. Matson recognized him as one of the cowboys from the Triangle T.

The man was short and thickset, in his late fifties, with greying hair and alert dark eyes. His voice was quiet but assured. 'My name's Walt Carter. I saw yuh come in, Mr Matson.' He hesitated for a moment. Then he smiled, half-apologetically. 'I hear tell yuh had a run-in with a feller called Murkin — Lance Murkin.'

'Yuh know him?' Matson's interest was aroused at once.

'Better than most. I rode with him fer an outfit north of here, at Bender's Creek, years ago. But he was buildin' himself a herd — with his boss's cattle, an' I quit.' The man paused. 'I ain't ever seen him since, but two of his pards from that outfit are well known in Baronsley — Matthew Ingham an' Rick Pallas.'

Matson's senses told him that another piece of the jigsaw was about to click into place. He said quietly, but with a smile, 'An' yuh don't reckon any o' those three as buddies, Mr Carter?'

Carter shook his head. 'Ingham an' Pallas were in cahoots with Murkin. Still are, I guess.'

'An' Deken an' Jefferson?'

Carter frowned. 'Both work fer Ingham. Have done fer some time. Though he sorta keeps 'em under cover. Mind yuh, no one ain't ever seen 'em workin'.'

Matson hesitated. Then he said, 'An' Bush?'

A voice from behind the tree inquired, almost gently, 'What's your interest in him, Matson?'

The tall figure of Nelson Bush stepped out into the open.

16

Luke Matson looked at Bush. There was a sombre look in the man's eyes, and his face was taut with decision, as though he had fought a hard battle with himself and won.

The deputy turned to Carter. 'You've been a great help, Walt. I want yuh to ride over to the Triangle and ask Mr Tate if he can spare another half-dozen men over here fer a day or two. Tell him I reckon we'll know who's behind the killings, an' why, by then.'

The grey-haired cowpuncher was gone almost before Matson finished speaking. The deputy spoke to Nelson Bush, now standing quietly at his side. 'We weren't expectin' yuh back fer another two or three days, Mr Bush.'

It was then that he remembered the conversation with Bush's hotel clerk. And he was certain now that his guess about the identity of this man had been correct.

He said quietly, 'Only, your name ain't Bush. You're Barton's eldest son — Warren Barton. Ain't that so?'

'I ain't denyin' it. But I had to git back,' said Barton bluntly. 'I'm the only one who can stop another killin'.'

'Supposin' yuh start at the beginnin',' suggested Matson.

The hotel owner shrugged. 'I got mixed up with Ingham when I was a youngster. He gave me a job. It meant breakin' the law, but I finally broke away when he wanted to teach me bushwhacking. He found me here about a couple of years ago; I had jest bought the hotel. He also knew my real name, an' that I had been given a hell of a lot o' money — with a ranch to come. An' he said he would turn me over to the law — which he could have done — if I didn't join up with him again.'

'Then what were yuh supposed to do?' asked Matson.

'Nothin',' said Barton. 'Jest wait until my old man died, then sell Ingham the ranch — at his price.' He looked at Matson. 'Ingham wanted to have the ol' man killed then an' there. I drew the line at that, an' Ingham finally gave in. But it cost me plenty.'

'An' then,' said Matson quietly, 'yuh found out that yuh had a half-brother?'

Warren Barton nodded. 'My father's lawyer found out where I was, an' wrote an' told me. I agreed to share the ranch — an' made up my mind to break from Ingham again, and fer good this time.'

Matson looked keenly at the tall man. 'An' then?'

Barton matched his gaze without flinching. 'The killings started. I hadn't been told my half-brother's name at that time, but when he was bushwhacked Ingham came into the hotel an' boasted that Felix had been shot, an' I wouldn't have to share the ranch now. It turned out that the lawyer was in Ingham's pay an' had got in touch with him. There was also someone else behind Ingham. An' this man had got himself a job with my father — as his *segundo* an' personal bodyguard.'

'Lance Murkin,' said Matson.

Warren Barton nodded. 'Yes. Then I knew. If they killed Felix Wilson, my ol' man would be next. An' no way would they let me live once I had sold Ingham or Murkin the ranch.'

Luke Matson took off his badge. 'I'm goin' to ask yuh another question,' he said. 'If yuh answer it truthfully, it'd probably be my duty as a lawman to arrest yuh. But I reckon if I ain't wearin' my badge it'll be safe fer yuh to talk. What d'yuh say?'

Barton thought for a moment, then he nodded. 'Yuh want to know what hold Ingham has over me. Right?'

'It would help,' said Matson. 'I can't promise, but Sheriff Stephens is a reasonable sort o' man. But these killings have come to haunt him lately. We've had nothin' to go on at all. But, with what you've told me, things could be comin' to a head, could even be cleared up. An' that could mean a clean slate an' a fresh start fer yuh.'

'I'll take my chance,' said Barton quietly, and for a moment Matson could see the likeness between the hotel owner and Felix Wilson, and their link with James Barton.

Warren Barton hesitated for a long moment.

Matson waited patiently.

Finally, Barton said slowly, 'Ingham an' five more put a couple o' tree trunks across the railroad east o' Bender's Creek. I was seventeen then an' wild. I had the job o' lookin' after the horses. Ingham an' the other four boarded the train, but some feller lookin' fer glory headed fer me. He drew his six-gun an' fired. I had no choice. I fired back an' he dropped. Next thing I knew, Ingham an' the rest were jumpin' off the train. They'd had a good haul. But a week later Ingham told me the law was after me, an' I would surely hang if they caught me. He said there was a poster with my name on it, an' that was that.'

'Was the feller yuh shot, dead?'

'I don't know. He never moved after I fired. But dead or not, I'd have hanged.'

There was no doubt about that, thought Matson. He said, 'Yuh willin' to accept Pat Stephens's action on what you've jest told me?'

'I'll go along with that.' Warren Barton's features seemed to have lightened with his words. He looked Matson full in the face. 'D'yuh know what made me make up my mind?'

'Tell me,' invited Matson.'

'Felix Wilson bein' shot down, an' the sight of Pete Connors dead outside the livery stable. That I couldn't stomach.'

'Yuh got any idea who killed Pete, or John Wilson, or ol' Billy Welch?'

Matson saw the pain in the suddenly not so hard blue eyes as Barton answered. 'I ain't certain. Ingham was clever. He talked up a feud between Wilson an' Pallas until the whole town believed it. Then he brought in Deken an' Jefferson an' hid them fer a while.

Jefferson is a knife man. I reckon he killed John Wilson an' Billy Welch — but there's no proof. Deken would rather kill than eat. He was seen near the livery stable when Connors was killed, but everyone's scared to talk.'

'An' what about your father?'

'I swore I'd never see him again. I guess I was born jest as stubborn as him. I've come to realize deep down that he was tough on me fer my own good. It was only stupid pride that stopped me seein' him again — an' I regret it.'

He stopped and was silent. Then he said, 'Finally, I had a run-in with Ingham, when he told me that a few days before his death Connors had overheard him an' Pallas talkin' about me an' my father, an' realized who I was. Connors even went to Ingham to check on it. The poor devil had signed his own death warrant. I decided to leave Baronsley fer a few days to sort myself out.'

Matson made up his mind. 'I've got to git back to Baronsley,' he said. 'But yuh ain't goin' to be safe there if Ingham even half suspects that yuh're ready to give yourself up.' He thought for a moment. 'Yuh heard me send to Andrew Tate fer more help here. I reckon yuh should stay here as well. With you an' Felix Wilson, an' nine Triangle hands, this ranch could handle any trouble.'

He didn't mention the presence of James Barton — he had a hunch that a surprise meeting after all these years might be the best for both Bartons.

Warren Barton nodded briefly. He was at Matson's side as the deputy entered the house and walked into the living-room.

Felix Wilson, James Barton, Janet Wilson and her mother looked up as the door opened. At the sight of Matson's companion, James Barton's eyes widened in amazement, and his hands clutched the top of the table for support.

At his side, Matson heard Warren Barton draw in his breath sharply as the old man stared unbelievingly at him.

17

Luke Matson arrived back in Baronsley late that afternoon. To his surprise, people looked up almost furtively as he rode towards the sheriff's office, some even turning and staring as though he was an unwelcome intruder in their midst, a stranger with no purpose in the town. He counted, he reckoned, as many scowls as smiles.

The sheriff was not in his office. On the table was a note. 'Luke, it's half-past four. Bud Jenning has sent for help. I'm going now.'

Matson looked at the clock. It was now nearly five. He crossed the room to the window overlooking Main Street. There seemed to be more people about than usual at this hour. He picked a shotgun from the rack, loaded it and stuffed extra shells in his pocket.

As he neared the Lucky Chance he

could hear voices raised inside the saloon. He stopped outside the batwing doors. The voices died away, until only one was left. The voice was Ingham's. He transferred the shotgun from his left hand to his right and pushed through the doors.

His entrance seemed to be unnoticed. The customers crowding the room were motionless, intense, gazing fixedly at the bar. Behind the counter a stony-faced Bud Jenning and the sheriff faced a group of men. In their centre swaggered Ingham and Rick Pallas, together with Deken and Jefferson.

Ingham's voice was now a shout. 'You're useless, Stephens. Innocent folk in this town are afraid to walk the streets. How many more are goin' to be killed before yuh do somethin' to earn your money?'

The sheriff remained silent, but Matson was sure that both he and the barkeep had seen him come in. He shook his head as a warning as he continued to make his way through the silent onlookers until he was standing unseen behind Ingham.

But it was Rick Pallas who brought the sheriff to his feet, white-faced in anger.

'Why don't yuh quit, Stephens? You're too old fer the job, an' mebbe that hash-slingin' woman o' yours'll be stupid enough to keep yuh fer the rest o' your miserable days.'

Stephens came round the bar counter in one move, yanked Pallas bodily from the centre of his friends, hit him twice with sledgehammer blows to the chin and then sunk his fists into the gunman's stomach.

Pallas gasped, hit the floor, twitched, and lay still.

The silence that followed was shattered by a triumphant yell from Ingham as his hand flashed to his gunbelt, 'You're dead, Stephens!'

With his left hand, Matson pressed the shotgun muzzle deep into the fat of Ingham's neck. 'If yuh fancy havin' your head separated from your body, go ahead an' draw.'

Ingham stiffened.

Matson leaned forward and drew the fat man's gun from its holster. 'Turn round, slowly,' he said. 'My trigger finger's a mite itchy.'

A white-faced Ingham obeyed him.

Sheriff Stephens bent down and disarmed the prostrate Pallas. Matson threw him Ingham's forty-five.

The deputy then waved the shotgun in the direction of Deken and Jefferson. His voice was icy. 'You two have got a choice. Make your move or shuck your hardware.'

In the room a man coughed nervously.

Jefferson snarled, unbuckled his belt, and let it fall.

There was a fixed smile on Deken's face. His fingers twitched, white-knuckled, inches from his belt.

Matson looked deep into the slim gunman's eyes, sighed, and tossed the shotgun to the sheriff. 'Keep an eye on the others, Pat.'

The sudden move seemed to take

Deken by surprise. He hesitated.

Matson half-turned to face him, relaxed, hands easy at his side. He said, 'Yuh won't find me as easy to kill as Pete Connors. Well?'

Deken's smile had disappeared. He said hoarsely, 'How the Devil did yuh — ? Damn yuh, lawman! No one gits the drop on me twice.'

Matson looked at the beads of sweat trickling down the other man's face, and said again, 'Well?'

Deken yelled and his right hand swooped down to his belt, the fingers closing round the butt of his six-gun, sweeping the weapon out of its holster in a blindingly fast surge of speed.

But there was a disbelieving gasp from the onlookers as Matson drew and fired twice, in one smooth, split-second faster, movement.

Deken seemed to hang motionless, his feet off the ground, mouth fixed in a grimace, while the crowd gasped again as blood pumped through the fingers of the hand that clutched spasmodically at his chest. Then his body slumped slowly forward, face downward on the saloon floor.

Matson, his face a mask, stood silent, forty-five in hand. His eyes searched the crowd, and men shivered at his look.

Then from behind him, Pat Stephens said quietly, 'Come back, stranger. The killing's over. Put the gun away, Luke.'

For a moment, Matson looked at the sheriff without seeing him, shaking his head stiffly, struggling to block out a disturbing picture. At last the shadows faded from his mind; he holstered his forty-five, hesitated, then turned to where the sheriff stood at the bar.

Without a word, Bud Jenning pushed a glass of whiskey towards him.

Matson nodded his thanks and drained the glass.

The sheriff said apologetically, 'Fer a moment yuh were so far away I didn't recognize yuh, Luke.' He waited while the barkeep refilled the deputy's glass. 'An' I sure didn't know Deken was that fast.'

Matson hardly heard him. He watched Ingham and Pallas slink away, followed by Jefferson and half a dozen men carrying Deken's body with them.

The sheriff said, 'I'm glad yuh got my message, Luke. Things were lookin' a trifle uncertain until yuh turned up with the scatter-gun. What else's been happenin'?'

This time Matson turned and looked at the two men. Both the sheriff and Bud Jenning had a look of concern in their eyes, as though they were puzzled by his silence, but were not quite sure what to do about it. He looked around the room. There were still several customers left, drinking or playing cards, among them men he recognized as friends of Ingham and Pallas. He said quietly, 'A lot's been happenin', Pat. I'll tell yuh back at the office. An' Bud, thanks fer givin' us your support. A pity there weren't that many more citizens keen on helpin'.'

At the batwing doors he pushed through ahead of Stephens, hand close to his forty-five. But the street was empty.

*   *   *

Later, in the office, the sheriff listened while his deputy spoke of his journey to the Bar W with James Barton, and his meeting with the rancher's son. 'An' yuh reckon that Bush — or Warren Barton, as we should call him — has split from Ingham fer good?'

Matson said, 'I'd stake my life on it. An' he's willin' to put himself in your hands when it's all over.'

Stephens frowned. 'If he killed a lawman to avoid capture, there ain't nothin' I can do fer him. But Ingham said there was a poster out with the boy's name on it, an' the law wanted him. Now, Warren Barton didn't say if the feller he shot was wearin' a star; he didn't know if he was dead; an' he didn't say if he ever saw the poster himself.'

The sheriff opened a drawer in his

desk. He pulled out a bundle of papers. 'Twenty years ago, yuh said? Near Bender's Creek?'

He shuffled through the crumpled posters, stopping every now and then for a closer examination. Finally, he shook his head. 'Nothin' fer that area at that time. It ain't likely that Warren Barton killed a man that day, but I'll do another check later on, jest to make sure.'

'Young Barton was jest seventeen at the time, an' it looks like he was fed a passel o' lies. He would've had no chance against a man like Ingham,' said Matson.

'He won't stand much chance now,' said the sheriff, drily. 'Ingham has lost control of him — which means his bluff's no longer workin'. Warren Barton knows too much. The one thing Ingham's got to do is silence him.'

'Hell!' Matson jumped to his feet. 'If he's thinkin' o' killing Warren Barton, he'll have to kill his father first. Otherwise he'll never git his hands on the Barton ranch.'

'Yuh an' me are payin' the Bar W a visit pronto,' said the sheriff. 'Warren Barton owns the Baronsley Hotel, which makes him a resident, an' entitled to the protection o' the law.' He laughed. 'If Ingham finds out you an' me are both out o' town, he's liable to try an' make trouble about that, too.'

Matson thought for a moment. 'That's a point. Let's bring everyone from the Bar W back here, tomorrow mornin',' he said. 'You stay here. I'll ride over now to the Triangle an' fix it with Andrew Tate. We shan't want his riders fer long. Tonight I'll stop over at the Bar W. Tomorrow Ingham an' Murkin'll have to make their play at once when they see the Bartons an' Wilsons ride in together.' Provided, of course, that they are prepared to ride in together, he thought.

★　★　★

At the Triangle T, Andrew Tate was enthusiastic. 'If yuh reckon yuh can git this affair settled soon, yuh can take every hand I've got,' he said. He looked keenly at Matson. 'One o' my men was in the Lucky Chance earlier this evenin'. He reckons yuh gave that gunslick Deken a choice an' he chose the wrong one.'

Matson shrugged. 'The bar was packed with Ingham's men, an' there was no way the sheriff an' me could back down. Deken wasn't fast enough, an' that was the end o' the trouble.'

Tate nodded. Then he looked searchingly at the deputy. 'What are yuh plannin' to do when this affair is over, Luke?'

Matson looked as keenly at the older man. 'My wanderin' days are over,' he said. 'I jest want to stay here. In peace. Fer the rest o' my life.'

A voice from the doorway spoke softly. 'Am I part of the rest of your life, Luke?'

The deputy turned slowly. Susan Tate came towards him, her brown eyes smiling, face uplifted to his. He took her in his arms. 'Not jest a part, my love. The whole of it.'

'That's nice,' she said. 'Wholly satisfactory.' She half-turned her head and looked at her father. 'What do you think, Dad?'

Andrew Tate was at the open door. He swung round and smiled at his daughter. 'Yuh look jest like your mother did, all those years ago,' he said. His smile widened. 'An' jest like her, yuh show good sense.'

The door closed softly behind him.

18

An hour before sun-up Luke Matson headed a score of riders as they left the Bar W on their way into Baronsley. Felix Wilson, Warren Barton, and James Barton, together with Martha and Janet Wilson, followed him. The Triangle T ranch-hands, with Andrew Tate and his daughter, rode silently in single file in the rear. To avoid detection the party took a little-used trail on the eastern side of Andrew Tate's range that would bring them into Baronsley near the hotel. The town seemed to be wrapped in sleep as they entered.

At a word from Matson, Warren Barton dismounted at the livery stable and disappeared round the corner of the building. A minute later the door of the stable opened and he reappeared. One by one the ranch-hands rode in, dismounted, and came out again, leaving two men with the horses. Then the party crossed the street and entered the hotel, followed by the sheriff, who had been waiting for them.

The hotel clerk jumped to his feet when Warren Barton, the sheriff and Matson appeared at the reception desk. 'Johnson,' said Barton, 'git over to the Bull an' tell Matthew Ingham I'm back an' want to see him.'

The clerk reached the door.

'An' Johnson,' said Barton.

The clerk turned round.

'I'm on my own. Got that?'

The clerk nodded, and closed the door behind him.

Matson grinned at the hotel keeper. 'Yuh reckon Ingham will come?'

Barton's voice was grim. 'He'll come. Probably to kill me. I know too much.'

Matson looked at him. He had discovered that the Bartons and Wilsons had had a surprisingly comfortable meeting at the Bar W. Martha Wilson, in particular, had been ready to forget the troubles of the past, especially when James Barton promised her that the men who had killed her husband and wounded her adopted son would be hounded down. And Felix Wilson and Warren Barton had found themselves in agreement with her.

At that moment the clerk returned.

'Well?' asked Barton.

The clerk shook his head. 'Mr Ingham ain't there,' he said. 'Ain't nobody there. The barkeep reckons that Mr Ingham an' that friend o' his — Mr Murkin — an' a heap o' others rode out round about daybreak today. He said they were goin' to pay the Bar W a visit, an' it wouldn't be a friendly one either.'

The sheriff said, 'It ain't goin' to take 'em long to figger out what's happened. They'll be hightailin' it back here any time now.' He was silent for a moment. 'We've got plenty o' Winchesters an' forty-fives. Me, I've got a hankerin' fer a shotgun. Allus comes in handy at times like this.'

Matson watched as the sheriff crossed the street to his office. The deputy smiled at the sight. Pat Stephens was whistling quietly to himself, his features relaxed, the tension and worry of the past few days gone now as he prepared for action.

It was easy enough to conceal the ranch-hands in the hotel's upper rooms, facing the street, with the women safe in one of the rooms below. But Felix Wilson and Warren Barton and their father insisted on joining Luke Matson and Andrew Tate at the hotel entrance.

Then as they waited, they heard the murmur of voices and the street seemed to be filling with people heading in their direction. Matson recognized a familiar figure among the leaders. It was Josey Simmonds. As she saw him, she turned and came across to the hotel entrance.

Her face was troubled. 'Luke,' she said, 'What's going on? Ingham and that rabble of his rode out of town earlier. Folk say he was heading for the Bar W and a showdown with you, and then he was coming back here,

215

threatening to make sure Baronsley needed a new sheriff. Where is Pat, Luke? I'm worried. I've got to warn him.'

Matson looked at her anxious face. And then he smiled. 'Over there, Josey,' he said, and pointed across the street.

The familiar figure of the sheriff was even then coming towards them, nursing a shotgun in his arms.

Josey's features were a mixture of pleasure and fear.

Matson said quietly, 'He's a big man, Josey. An' he's doin' the job he knows best.'

She sighed. Then she said, hands clenched tight, 'I found that out just in time, Luke. I'm not figuring on stopping him. I just want to be near him.'

Matson said, 'Stay here, Josey. Pat'll be glad to know you're with us. Martha an' Janet Wilson an' Susan are inside. They'll be happy fer yuh to join them.'

She smiled at the deputy. 'Just tell him I'm here and I'll be waiting for him, Luke.' She turned and made her way through the door.

As she disappeared, Luke watched as the sheriff came to a halt in the middle of the street. Stephens's voice was loud and clear and directed at the crowd of curious onlookers, all apparently anxious to see what was going to happen.

'Go home,' he said. 'All of yuh. My deputy an' me have got a job to do. A job to finish. An' part of it is to make sure that none of yuh git hurt. So go home now, an' don't come out again until it's safe.'

Matson felt a sense of pride and respect as he watched the lawman stand silent and relaxed, facing the crowd, as they, in ones and twos, then in groups, drifted as silently away.

Not until the last one disappeared did the sheriff turn and join Matson and his companions.

The deputy said quietly, 'Josey's in the hotel with Susan an' the others, Pat. Ingham's been boastin' that Baronsley's due fer a new sheriff, an' she came to warn yuh.' He let his voice drop so only the sheriff could hear. 'Said she jest wanted to be near yuh.'

He watched as the sheriff's weather-beaten face softened at the mention of Josey. Then that face hardened again as the sound of horses approaching at a gallop filled the air.

'It's you an' me, Luke,' said the lawman softly, and together they stepped into the middle of the street. Matson was conscious of movement, and out of the corner of his eye saw Andrew Tate, together with James Barton and his sons, line up behind them.

Down the middle of the thoroughfare swept a score of horsemen, clouds of dust almost blotting out Ingham and the tall figure of Murkin in their centre.

It was Ingham who first saw them and let out a triumphant yell as the leading horsemen reined in within yards of the sheriff and his shotgun, now levelled menacingly.

'Git down, Ingham!' ordered the

sheriff. 'Or I'll cut yuh in half!'

Ingham took one look at Sheriff Stephens's stony face and clambered down from the saddle.

Luke Matson had drawn his forty-five. He looked at Murkin, now on foot with Ingham, and at Jefferson and Pallas, still on horseback. 'I'll gut-shoot the first o' you three who makes a wrong move,' he observed pleasantly.

Murkin snarled at him, 'I'm not Jimmy Deken. I'll make my move at my own time.'

Matson was still smiling when he turned his attention on Jefferson. The big man stood staring at him, stiffly upright, his gnarled hands twisting together uneasily. Under Matson's gaze his eyes dropped.

'What are yuh worried about, Jefferson?' inquired Matson, his smile chilling at the edges. 'You're out in the open now among friends. Not in ol' Billy Welch's cabin, waitin' until he turns round so yuh can knife him in the back.'

Jefferson's mouth opened, and then

shut again at once as the deputy continued.

'Yea. You're out in the open. Not in the room where John Wilson is in bed, helpless, unable to move as yuh slip a knife between his ribs. Yuh're a brave *hombre*, Jefferson. Clever, too. So clever yuh managed to kill the wrong man — yuh thought he was Felix Wilson.'

He paused.

The men around the hotel entrance stood transfixed, as though they were waiting and wondering what was to come.

Jefferson stood bowed and shaking. Slowly his right hand came up over his ear, and he turned his face away from his accuser as though he could stand no more.

Matson watched in silence. When he spoke, his voice was harsh. 'Yuh killed two men in cold blood — one old an' helpless, the other sick an' helpless — fer a few dollars. How much were yuh paid, Jefferson?'

Jefferson licked his lips, and tried to speak but failed. He seemed to scratch the back of his neck with his right hand, as though in confusion, and then struggled upright. His hand swooped and flashed forward.

There was a glint of steel.

Felix Wilson yelled a warning.

19

Felix Wilson's yell was answered by the blast of Matson's forty-five. The slug hit Jefferson's wrist, shattering it, and a black-handled knife spun to the ground.

Matson turned on him, the forty-five aimed unerringly at his belt buckle.

Jefferson sank to his knees, clutching his bloodstained wrist with his left hand. 'Don't shoot,' he pleaded.

'Why shouldn't I?' Matson crouched over him, forty-five rammed into the man's stomach. 'If yuh want to live to be hanged, start talkin'. Who killed Pete Connors an' bushwhacked John an' Felix Wilson?'

Jefferson screamed as the forty-five sunk in further. Then he moaned, 'Jimmy Deken. I had nothin' to do with it.'

The deputy said savagely, 'Keep talkin' — loud an' clear. Who knifed

Billy Welch an' John Wilson?'

There was silence for a moment.

'Well?' rasped Matson.

'I did,' muttered Jefferson.

'Louder,' insisted Matson. 'My friends didn't hear yuh.'

'I did,' admitted Jefferson.

'Who d'yuh work fer?' asked Matson.

Jefferson said hesitantly, 'Matthew Ingham.'

'He pays yuh?'

'Yes.'

There was a defiant shout from Ingham. 'He's a liar. I ain't standin' any more o' this. What are yuh fellers waitin' fer? There's enough of us here to wipe out Stephens an' his deputy an' the rest of 'em.'

'Mebbe so,' the voice of the sheriff put in. 'But there ain't enough of 'em to stop me blastin' yuh with this here scatter-gun if one of 'em decides to accept your invitation.'

The sheriff glanced across at Luke, and then back at Ingham. 'There's another reason why your men ain't goin' to do any shootin' today,' he said. 'Tell 'em, Luke.'

The deputy looked up. 'I reckon Mr Tate's the man fer that job,' he said.

Andrew Tate stepped forward. He looked at Ingham and Murkin and the men with them, and shook his head. 'The town don't need yuh,' he said.

'An' the ranchers don't need yuh either. An' I've got a score o' reasons here to back up what the sheriff jest said.' He turned his back on Ingham. 'Show yourselves, boys!'

As he spoke, his men appeared at the hotel windows, Winchesters levelled.

For a minute there was a hush. Then, one by one, at a sign from the sheriff, Ingham's men unbuckled their gun-belts, let them fall, and slunk away.

Only Ingham himself, Murkin and his two companions from James Barton's ranch, the wounded Jefferson, and Rick Pallas remained outside the hotel, facing the sheriff and his men.

The sheriff stared at the fat man. 'I don't fancy dirtyin' my jail with the likes o' you, Ingham,' he said. 'But yuh gave blood-money to Jefferson an' Deken fer three innocent men's lives an' now you're goin' to pay.'

Ingham sneered at him. 'Yuh ain't got no real evidence, lawman. I've got one o' the finest lawyers in the country in my pocket. Your two-bit jail won't hold me fer a week.'

'You're yaller, Ingham,' said a bitter voice.

Felix Wilson stepped out into the centre of the street. Matson opened his mouth, but at the look on the young man's face he left the warning unsaid.

'You're yaller, Ingham,' Wilson said again. 'Yuh hid behind two no-account killers an' now you're figgerin' on hidin' behind a cheap lawyer. Why are yuh wearin' a forty-five, Ingham? I reckon it'd be too heavy fer yuh to lift — on your own.'

There was a burst of laughter from the onlookers.

But that stung Ingham into action. 'Damn yuh to hell, Wilson,' he yelled, and his right hand swooped down to his gunbelt.

But fast as he was, his forty-five never cleared leather. Felix Wilson's Colt bucked in his hand three times, and each slug found its target. Blood poured from a hole in Ingham's chest, but as the fat man slumped to the floor both hands were clawing at his slowly reddening stomach.

Wilson stood over him and watched pitilessly as the man's eyes filmed over. 'John Wilson can sleep in peace, now,' he said, his voice flat. 'But you never will.'

★   ★   ★

Sheriff Stephens sat in his chair, a glass of whiskey in his hand, feet comfortably up on his desk. He grinned at his deputy, sitting opposite him.

Matson lifted his glass to him. 'If yuh had told me, a couple of hours ago, how quiet this town would be this afternoon — I wouldn't have believed it,' he said.

226

The sheriff drained his glass. 'By the way, I got word from Bender's Creek yesterday. Seems there was never a Wanted poster fer a *hombre* called Nelson Bush, all those years ago. But there was one fer Matthew Ingham — fer unlawful shootin' of a law officer. So Warren Barton's in the clear. An' I told him so. Hell, he gave us the breakthrough we needed, jest at the right time, an' as far as I'm concerned, he's put the record straight.'

The deputy put his now-empty glass down. 'It worries me some,' he said. 'But my memory ain't what it was. Nelson Bush? I can't remember a Nelson Bush nohow. Ain't no one o' that name in Baronsley, anyhow.'

The sheriff stood up and reached for his Stetson. 'Yuh'll make a good lawman yet,' he said. 'A fast draw goes with the job — but a shaky memory can help the cause o' justice more at times.' He shook his head. 'Hell. I've plumb forgotten what I jest said.'

'I've jest watched yuh forgit it,' said Matson.

The office door opened and Warren Barton and Felix Wilson came in.

The sheriff glanced at the clock. 'Nice to see yuh boys,' he said. 'But yuh've only got two minutes. Luke an' me has work to do.'

'Must be terrible hard bein' a sheriff,' said Warren Barton.

'Official business. Can't stop an' discuss it right now.' The sheriff reached the door, followed by the deputy — and Barton and Wilson.

'We'll walk along with yuh an' discuss it,' said Warren Barton. 'There's talk in the Lucky Chance that you've given Murkin an' Pallas, an' Murkin's two sidekicks, till five o'clock to leave town.'

'That's in about three minutes,' said Felix Wilson. 'An' folk were sorta suggestin' that two younger men — with better eyesight — ought to go along with our agein' sheriff an' his younger an' inexperienced deputy, jest to make sure that Murkin an' his pards

228

have really crossed the town boundaries.'

'I am orderin' you two to go back,' said the sheriff, with, thought Matson, the air of a man who hasn't much chance of being obeyed.

Wilson and Barton retreated until they were a full two paces behind the sheriff.

'We can catch up with the ol' feller anytime,' said Felix Wilson to his companion.

By now they had reached the Spanish Bull. The sheriff turned round. 'All right,' he said. 'We're goin' in. You two — one on each side of the door, an' keep your eyes skinned.'

Matson was the first inside. The room was empty, except for the barkeep cowering behind his bar. Matson reached him. 'Where's Murkin?' he demanded.

Sweat stood out on the barkeep's face. He shook his head.

Matson drew his forty-five. 'I ain't got time to argue,' he said. 'Where's Murkin?'

The man licked his lips nervously. 'I ain't tellin',' he whispered. 'He'll kill me fer sure.' His eyes looked furtively to his left for an instant.

Matson waited. The sheriff stood on his left, forty-five drawn. The deputy turned slowly and looked in the direction the barkeep had indicated. Behind the bar, steps led upwards, with curtains drawn across them halfway up. As he watched, he saw a movement behind the curtains. He stiffened.

But at that moment, the barkeep, face panic-stricken, dropped down clumsily behind his bar.

Lance Murkin emerged through the curtains. He stood motionless on the steps, hands poised just above his gunbelt. He looked at Matson.

'Yuh're out o' time, Murkin,' said the deputy. 'Drop your gunbelt. You're goin' to jail.'

'An' you're goin' to hell,' sneered Murkin. 'Git out o' my way, lawman!' He yelled, and his hand flashed down to his forty-five.

But even as Murkin's fingers closed around the butt of the Colt, the roar of Matson's levelled forty-five blasted the sudden hush in the bar-room. For a moment, Murkin seemed to hang in the air as blood spurted wildly from a hole in his chest. Then he collapsed, to fall in a disjointed heap at Matson's feet.

The deputy looked at the body once, and then turned to where the barkeep leaned white-faced on the bar. 'Pallas, an' Murkin's two *compadres*, where are they?' he demanded.

The barkeep swallowed nervously. 'They left a couple of hours ago,' he said. 'They reckoned they didn't want to face the feller who downed Jimmy Deken, an' so they lit out.'

Matson nodded. He noticed that he was alone with the barkeep. He pushed his way through the batwing doors and out into the hard sunlight. There was no sign of Warren Barton or Felix Wilson, but the sheriff was there. At his side Josey Simmonds smiled up at him, the happiness in her face mirrored in his.

Matson felt suddenly alone and empty. Then he heard soft footsteps behind him, and turned. Susan Tate walked into his arms. There were tears in her eyes and he felt her body shaking.

'The sheriff told me,' she whispered. 'Lance Murkin tried to kill you.'

'Hush, my love,' he said. 'There'll be no more killin'. The past is behind us. Now we've got the rest of today to start the rest of our life.'

THE END

We do hope that you have enjoyed reading this large print book.

Did you know that all of our titles are available for purchase?

We publish a wide range of high quality large print books including:
Romances, Mysteries, Classics
General Fiction
Non Fiction and Westerns

Special interest titles available in large print are:
The Little Oxford Dictionary
Music Book, Song Book
Hymn Book, Service Book

Also available from us courtesy of Oxford University Press:
Young Readers' Dictionary
(large print edition)
Young Readers' Thesaurus
(large print edition)

For further information or a free brochure, please contact us at:
Ulverscroft Large Print Books Ltd.,
The Green, Bradgate Road, Anstey,
Leicester, LE7 7FU, England.
Tel: (00 44) **0116 236 4325**
Fax: (00 44) **0116 234 0205**

A TOWN CALLED TROUBLESOME

John Dyson

Matt Matthews had carved his ranch out of the wild Wyoming frontier. But he had his troubles. The big blow of '86 was catastrophic, with dead beeves littering the plains, and the oncoming winter presaged worse. On top of this, a gang of desperadoes had moved into the Snake River valley, killing, raping and rustling. All Matt can do is to take on the killers single-handed. But will he escape the hail of lead?